westermann

W0239239

CAMDEN MARKET

9

Challenge-Heft

CAMDEN MARKET 9

Autor: Daniel Walker (Frankfurt am Main)
Unter Mitwirkung von: Demet Kömür
Fachliche Beratung: Cordula Dopichei, Bianka Gehler, Juliane Nietz

Zusatzmaterialien zu Camden Market 9

Materialien für Lehrerinnen und Lehrer
- Textbook für Lehrkräfte 9 (ISBN 978-3-14-149186-9)
- Materialien für Lehrkräfte 9 (ISBN 978-3-14-149187-6)
- Differenzierende Kopiervorlagen 9 (ISBN 978-3-14-149192-0)
- Lernerfolgskontrollen 9 (ISBN 978-3-14-149189-0)
- CD für Lehrkräfte 9 (ISBN 978-3-14-149190-6)
- DVD für Lehrkräfte 9 (ISBN 978-3-14-149191-3)
- Online-Diagnose zu Camden Market 9 www.onlinediagnose.de

Materialien für Schülerinnen und Schüler
- Textbook 9 (ISBN 978-3-14-149175-3)
- Workbook 9 (ISBN 978-3-14-149176-0)
- Interaktive Übungen 9 (ISBN 978-3-14-149370-2)
- Arbeitsbuch Inklusion 9 (ISBN 978-3-14-149178-4)
- Grammatiktrainer 9 (ISBN 978-3-14-149181-4)
- Wortschatztrainer 9 (ISBN 978-3-14-149394-9)

Das digitale Schulbuch und digitale Unterrichtsmaterialien für Schülerinnen und Schüler und für Lehrkräfte finden Sie in der BiBox – dem digitalen Unterrichtssystem passend zum Lehrwerk. Mehr Informationen über aktuelle Lizenzen finden Sie auf www.bibox.schule.

www.westermann.de/camden-market

westermann GRUPPE

Druck A[1] / Jahr 2024
Alle Drucke der Serie A sind im Unterricht parallel verwendbar.

Redaktion: James Gough, Doreen Klahold, Demet Kömür und Henriette Vahle
Vokabelanhang: Lisa Hambrecht, Turin
Illustrationen: Ulf Marckwort, Kassel
Umschlaggestaltung: LIO Design GmbH, Braunschweig
Layout: JANSSEN KAHLERT Design & Kommunikation GmbH, Hannover
Druck und Bindung: Westermann Druck GmbH, Georg-Westermann-Allee 66, 38104 Braunschweig

ISBN 978-3-14-**149179**-1

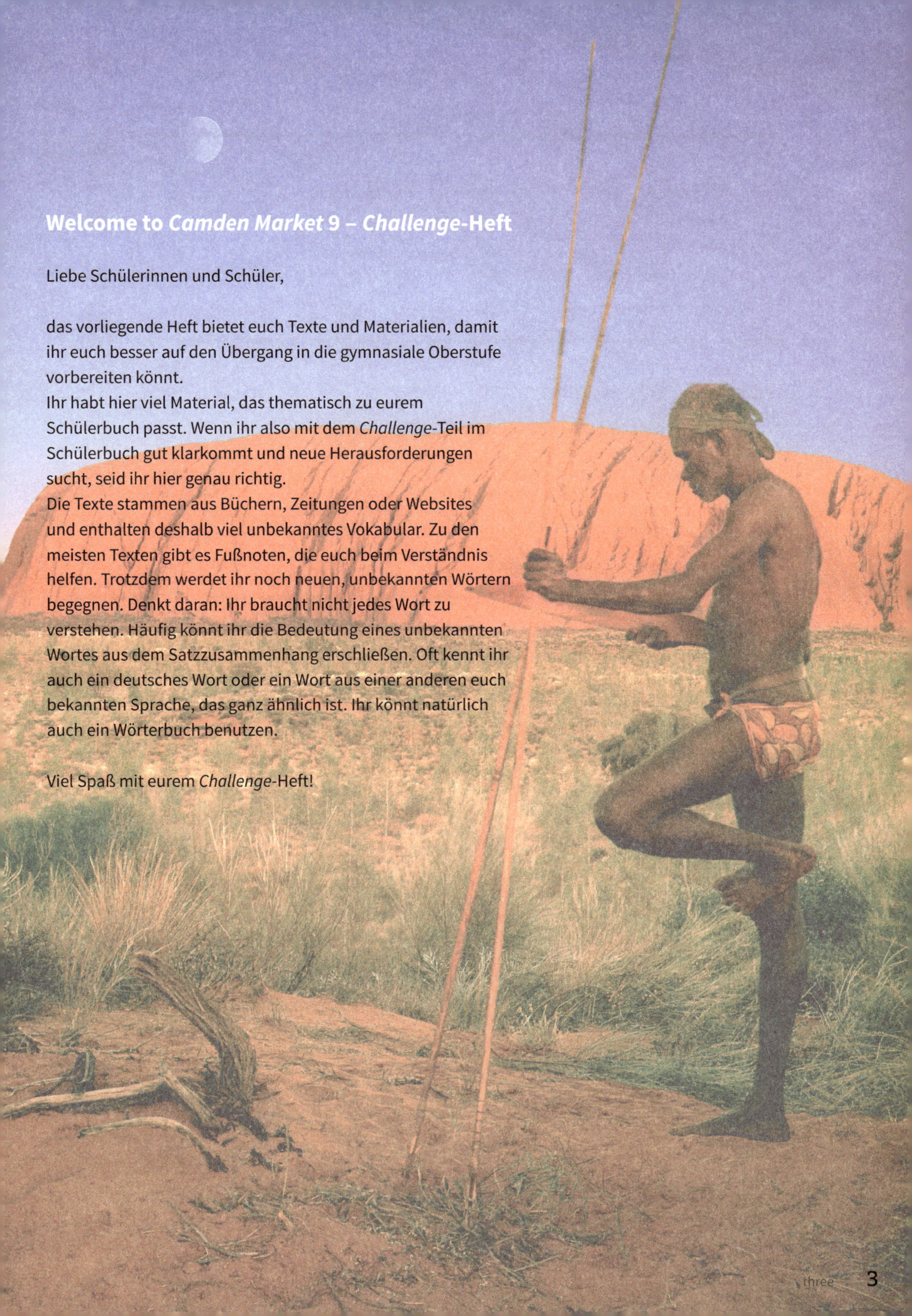

Welcome to *Camden Market* 9 – *Challenge*-Heft

Liebe Schülerinnen und Schüler,

das vorliegende Heft bietet euch Texte und Materialien, damit ihr euch besser auf den Übergang in die gymnasiale Oberstufe vorbereiten könnt.
Ihr habt hier viel Material, das thematisch zu eurem Schülerbuch passt. Wenn ihr also mit dem *Challenge*-Teil im Schülerbuch gut klarkommt und neue Herausforderungen sucht, seid ihr hier genau richtig.
Die Texte stammen aus Büchern, Zeitungen oder Websites und enthalten deshalb viel unbekanntes Vokabular. Zu den meisten Texten gibt es Fußnoten, die euch beim Verständnis helfen. Trotzdem werdet ihr noch neuen, unbekannten Wörtern begegnen. Denkt daran: Ihr braucht nicht jedes Wort zu verstehen. Häufig könnt ihr die Bedeutung eines unbekannten Wortes aus dem Satzzusammenhang erschließen. Oft kennt ihr auch ein deutsches Wort oder ein Wort aus einer anderen euch bekannten Sprache, das ganz ähnlich ist. Ihr könnt natürlich auch ein Wörterbuch benutzen.

Viel Spaß mit eurem *Challenge*-Heft!

INHALT

Die Angebote in *Camden Market* sind nicht linear abzuarbeiten.
Die Auswahl richtet sich nach den Schwerpunkten des schulinternen Curriculums.

INHALT

Die Aufgaben und Texte im *Challenge*-Heft sind den Themenschwerpunkten im Textbook (978-3-14-149175-3) zugeordnet. Der Verweis auf die passende Stelle im jeweiligen *Theme* ist in der Randspalte (**TB 12** p. 20) zu finden.

Die Lösungen zu den Aufgaben im *Challenge*-Heft können über ***www.westermann.de/webcode*** mit dem Webcode **WES-149179-001** abgerufen werden. Alternativ können Sie auch den **QR-Code** scannen:

TB 1 p. 4

1 Different Englishes

a) You know about British and American English. But there are many other "Englishes". Look at the dialogues. Where do you think the speakers are from?

b) Do some online research about different English expressions and ways of talking around the world. Explain what you found out.

In Scotland, people have many different words for …

2 The Commonwealth

TB PP p. 7

Read the article about the Commonwealth on page 8.
Use the different reading techniques from below.

a) Read the text and summarise[1] it in one or two sentences.

Skimming – reading for gist

1. If there are any photos or illustrations, look at them carefully.
2. Read the headings, photo captions[2] etc. They will give you clues[3] to what a text is about before you read it.
3. Read through the text quickly and in one go – don't stop to look up any new words, and concentrate on the gist[4], not the details.
4. After skimming the text, you can summarise in one or two sentences what it is about.

b) Scan the text for information about the members of the Commonwealth.
Take notes on:

- who the members are
- how many there are
- what their aims are.

Scanning – reading for information

1. Make sure you know exactly what information you are looking for.
   Go through the text slowly and note down keywords.
2. Read the sentences with the keywords, e.g. members.
   If there is additional information, take notes.
3. Don't worry about new words. Try to understand them from the context.

You have now used two different reading techniques – skimming and scanning. Before you read any text, think about what you want to find out and decide on your best reading strategy.

[1]summarise – *zusammenfassen*; [2]caption – *Bildunterschrift*; [3]clue – *Hinweis*; [4]the gist – *das Wesentliche*

The Commonwealth

The Commonwealth is an intergovernmental[1] organization consisting of many former[2] British colonies. In 1867 Canada was the first country in the British Empire to gain its independence[3]. Over the course[4] of the century that followed, most other colonies followed suit[5]. While their governments were independent of British rule most countries chose to nonetheless keep the British Monarch as their Head of State. These countries formed the British Commonwealth of Nations.
In 1949 the name was changed to simply the Commonwealth: this was to reflect the equal[6] status that the member countries enjoyed as member states.

Flag of the Commonwealth of Nations

Today the Commonwealth consists of 52 member states. There are countries from nearly every continent in the Commonwealth and its members include some of the largest and richest, as well as some of the smallest and poorest countries in the world. There is no formal constitutional structure, instead it is a voluntary association that works towards international goals. To do this, the association has several structured programmes that fall under the two broad categories of Democracy and Development. These programmes help to promote[7] significant values, such as Human Rights, peace and economic development within its member states. The principle of equality which the partnership is founded on is also behind the peaceful decolonization of its member states, as well as the fight against racism and promotion of sustainable development in poorer countries.

Each year, on the second Monday in March, Commonwealth Day is celebrated throughout the member states. The day is given a new theme each year and the British Monarch delivers a speech.

Many schools also get involved with the celebrations, participating[8] in various Commonwealth-related activities. Every four years, member states also have the chance to compete in the Commonwealth Games – a sporting event between all the countries, including some traditionally British sports, such as rugby, cricket and netball.

In 1999, Australia, one of the founding members[9] of the Commonwealth, held a referendum asking if Australia should remain in the Commonwealth, or if it should become a republic with an elected president as Head of State instead. Nearly 55% of voters[10] voted to remain in the Commonwealth, showing that there was still a loyalty to the British crown. Republicans in Australia would still like to sever ties[11] with the Commonwealth but the movement has lost enthusiasm in recent years.

[1]intergovernmental – *zwischenstaatlich*; [2]former – *ehemalig(e)*; [3]independence – *Unabhängigkeit*; [4]over the course – *im Lauf(e) des …*; [5]follow suit – *nachziehen, dasselbe machen*; [6]equal – *gleichberechtigt*; [7]promote sth – *etw fördern, für etw werben*; [8]participate (in sth) – *an etwas teilnehmen, sich an etw beteiligen*; [9]founding member – *Gründungsmitglied*; [10]voter – *Wähler/in*; [11]sever ties (with) – *sich von etw abkoppeln*

3 A global language

TB PP p. 7

a) Read the article. What do you find most interesting? Explain in one or two sentences.
I think it's interesting that the British Empire covered 24% of the Earth. …

English as a global language

By Tia Miller

At its peak[1], the British Empire was the largest empire in history. By 1913, the British Empire ruled[2] over 412 million people (23% of the world population at the time). By 1920, it covered 24% of the Earth's total land area. The phrase "the empire on which the sun never sets" was often used to describe the British Empire because its expanse[3] around the globe meant that the sun was always shining on at least one of its territories.
The process of decolonisation, beginning after World War II and arguably ending in 1997, caused the dissolution of the British Empire. However the political, legal, linguistic and cultural legacy[4] of it is still widespread.
British Imperialism went hand in hand with the spread of English as a global language. The first permanent English-speaking colony was in North America. Many others followed and today English is still the official language in 67 countries. Not surprisingly, the majority[5] of countries where English is an official language are former territories of the British Empire. Of course, English has spread much further. In total, about 1.36 billion people speak English. Only about 360 million of them are native speakers[6]. The others use English as a second language in their countries or have learned it as a foreign language and use it for business or pleasure. Asia, for example, is home to an estimated 350 million English-speakers: roughly the same number as in Britain, Canada and the USA combined. Despite the USA being the largest English-speaking country worldwide, only 20% of the world's English speakers live there. So the English language has been shared across the globe, 'belonging' to everyone. English is the common language in many aspects of modern life like science, air traffic control, shipping and so on. Even if you're not abroad or working, hardly a day goes by without seeing or hearing English; just switch on the radio or watch TV.
According to Walter Marks, professor of education at the University of California, Irvine, this is because the most common second language in the world is English. 'In many places, being able to speak English is a sign that you're educated[7]' he said.
English is increasingly being used in the domestic workplace too. As so much business – through the Internet as well as other methods of communication – is conducted in English, employees in some Swedish companies no longer even speak Swedish in the office.
This growth of English in the global economy is inextricably linked to globalization, the main culprit being the dominance of the USA and Britain in this area. A common language enables[8] countries to communicate across the world. The driving force behind the increased usage of English is the Internet, with more and more content being produced in it.
The only thing that might one day have the power to displace English as "lingua franca[9]" is technology. It may still be science-fiction, but one day you might have a button in your ear that translates the Urdu of your conversation partner directly into your mother tongue.

[1]peak – *Spitze, Höhepunkt*; [2]rule – *regieren*; [3]expanse – *Ausdehnung*; [4]legacy – *Vermächtnis, Erbe*; [5]majority – *Mehrheit*; [6]native speaker – *Muttersprachler/in*; [7]educated – *gebildet*; [8]enable – *befähigen, hier: ermöglichen*; [9]lingua franca – *Verkehrssprache, gemeinsame Sprache*

b) Answer the questions. Write down your answers.

1. When and why was the phrase "the empire on which the sun never sets" used?
2. How many countries have English as an official language?
3. Name at least two reasons why English is used in so many countries today.

c) Do you agree that "being able to speak English is a sign that you're educated"? Why? Why not? Write down your opinion.

4 Learning English

You have been studying English for a few years now.
Write a text about what you like about English and what you don't like about it.
Give examples of when you enjoyed using English or when it helped you to know English.

Writing

The different types of text you have to write all have their special characteristics.
What ever kind of text you write, you should still follow the basic principles of text writing.

These include the following phases:

A planning phase: collecting and organizing ideas for the task.
Before you start planning, it might be helpful to re-read that material and to note down useful ideas and thematic vocabulary and phrases you can use.

A drafting phase: outlining and writing a first draft.
Structure your ideas, e.g. add numbers to decide on the sequence.
Write a brief outline for your text using your notes from the planning phase.

An editing phase: correcting and improving your first draft and writing the "real" text.
Check the content and the language.

Make sure you leave yourself enough time at the end for the editing phase.

1 All about Australia

TB 2 p. 15

a) Read the text and make a fact file about Australia.

b) Use your fact file from a) and tell your class about the country.

Fact file about Australia
Official name: The Commonwealth of Australia
Other names: Down under, Oz
...

Australia is a country, an island and a continent. The official name is the Commonwealth of Australia. It includes the mainland of the Australian continent as well as the island of Tasmania and several smaller islands. In terms of[1] total area, it is the sixth largest country in the world. Germany is 63rd on the list!

Australia is quite a special place because it is the oldest, flattest and driest continent that people live on. It also has the least fertile[2] soils[3]. It has mountain ranges in the south-east, tropical rainforests in the north-east, and deserts in the middle, so you can say that its climate and landscapes are very diverse[4].

Australia has six neighbouring[5] countries: New Zealand to the south-east, the Solomon Islands and Vanuato to the north-east, and Papua New Guinea, Indonesia and East Timor to the north.

Australia has a federal parliament[6] which means that the country is divided into several states, like Germany. There are six states: New South Wales (NSW), Queensland (QLD), South Australia (SA), Tasmania (TAS), Victoria (VIC) and Western Australia (WA). It also consists of ten territories. Two of the major mainland territories are the Australian Capital Territory (ACT) and the Northern Territory (NT). The capital of Australia is Canberra which is in the ACT.

The population of Australia is nearly 26 million people. A large majority[7] of these people live in the east. The city with the biggest population is Sydney, which is also the financial centre of Australia. Melbourne, Brisbane, Perth and Adelaide are the next four largest cities. It is estimated that nearly 50% of the population have at least one parent who was born outside of Australia, with around 30% of the population being immigrants.

People sometimes use “Down under” to talk about Australia. That is because Australia is in the southern hemisphere[8] so Australia is at the bottom on a map. Another nickname is “Oz”. That comes from the international abbreviation[9] of Australia is AUS which is pronounced[10] “Oz”.

Australia’s flag contains[11] the colours blue, red and white. In the top-left corner, there is the Union Jack. This represents the history of British settlement in Australia. Below the Union Jack, there is a large white star with seven points. This is known as the Commonwealth Star. To the right, there are five white stars which represent the Southern Cross, a constellation[12] of five stars that you can see from the night skies of the southern hemisphere.

[1]in terms of – *bezüglich*; [2]fertile – *fruchtbar*; [3]soil – *Boden*; [4]diverse – *vielfältig, unterschiedlich*; [5]neighbouring – *benachbart*; [6]federal parliament – *Bundestag;* [7]majority – *Mehrheit*; [8]hemisphere – *(Erd)halbkugel, Hemisphäre*; [9]abbreviation – *Abkürzung*; [10]pronounce – *aussprechen*; [11]contain – *enthalten;* [12]constellation – *Sternbild*

TB 7 p. 17

2 The Great Barrier Reef

a) Read the text and find a title for each paragraph. Compare your ideas with a partner.

b) Sort the information about the Great Barrier Reef.
Think of location, size, age, animals, activities and other interesting facts.

c) Prepare a short talk about the Great Barrier Reef and present it.

Hundreds of brilliant colours, 14,000 kinds of life – all coming together in a fascinating area off the coast of Queensland in north-east Australia: That is the Great Barrier Reef, often simply called GBR. The Great Barrier Reef is the world's largest coral reef system composed of[1] over 2,900 individual reefs and 900 islands. It is the world's biggest single structure made by living organisms[2], which are known as coral polyps[3]. Polyps are tiny animals which join up[4] to form colonies. Each polyp lives inside a hard shell called coral. Millions of corals make up the reef. This "underwater[5] city" is so large (344,400 km^2) that it can be seen from outer space[6].

The Reef Research Centre has found the remains[7] of coral that they think are half a million years old. Researchers believe that coral has been growing in the area for up to 25 million years. The sea level[8] affects[9] the growth of a reef: On the one hand, coral needs sunlight to grow so it cannot grow in very deep water (150 metres or more). On the other hand, coral cannot grow above sea level either because it needs to be in the water. It is not easy to work out the exact age of the Great Barrier Reef. The Great Barrier Reef Marine Park Authority and Australian Institute of Marine Sciences estimate that the reef started growing around 20,000 years ago! They say that it started to grow on an older reef. These older reefs grew on hills on coastal[10] land which now forms the bottom of the Great Barrier Reef. As the sea level began to rise[11] from 20,000 years ago until 6,000 years ago, the coral started to grow higher on the hills. The Reef Research Centre estimates that the reef as we know it today is around 6,000 to 8,000 years old.

The Great Barrier Reef has been divided into 70 different areas. These are called bioregions and each bioregion has its own special plants and animals. There are 30 reef bioregions, and 40 are non-reef bioregions. In the northern part of the Great Barrier Reef, there are ribbon reefs and deltaic reefs. These kinds of reef do not exist in the rest of the Great Barrier Reef system.

It's not only the size and age of the Great Barrier Reef that is impressive[12]. It's the thousands of different kinds of sea life living together. The corals are constantly taking on[13] new forms to get more light. There are worms[14] that look like they are dancing. Millions of colourful, unusual and beautiful fish, including the parrotfish and the clownfish, live in the reef.

The GBR isn't just ideal for fish; it supports a wide range[15] of life. Six of the seven species of sea turtles[16], for example, come to the reef to breed[17]. The turtles are born there and hatch[18] from their eggs after several weeks. Then they swim into the sea but female sea turtles return after about 30 years to lay their own eggs. Sharks, whales, dolphins, snakes and even frogs call the reef their home. Many large colonies of birds nest on the islands of the Great Barrier Reef. About 1.7 million birds use the sites to breed. Because the GBR is so special, it was declared[19] a World Heritage Site[20] in 1981.

However, the reef is a very popular destination for tourists, especially in the Whitsunday Islands and Cairns region. Tourism is an important economic activity for the region. Australia quickly noticed the large interest and started offering tours in glass-bottomed boats, fishing tours, scuba diving and even helicopter flights[21] over the Great Barrier Reef. Because of this the water is getting dirtier and the corals can't grow properly. The natural balance[22] of life under the sea has been disturbed[23] by overfishing and souvenir divers.

But there is something that is even more of a problem to the Great Barrier Reef: coral bleaching. This is a result of increasing[24] sea water temperatures caused by global warming. So far, 2016 has been the worst year for the Great Barrier Reef and coral bleaching. Around two-thirds of a 700-km (435 miles) area of coral were killed in just nine months due to[25] high sea temperatures.

To protect this immense beauty, Australians now try to work with nature instead of destroying it. We humans must learn to develop a stronger sense of duty[26] towards our world and protect it.

[1]be composed of – *bestehen aus*; [2]living organism – *Lebewesen*; [3]polyp – *Polyp*; [4]join up – *sich verbinden*; [5]underwater – *Unterwasser-*; [6]outer space – *Weltall;* [7]remains – *Überreste*; [8]sea level – *Meeresspiegel*; [9]affect – *sich auswirken auf*; [10]coastal – *Küsten-*; [11]rise – *(auf/an)steigen;* [12]impressive – *beeindruckend;* [13]take on – *annehmen*; [14]worm – *Wurm*; [15]range – *Reichweite, hier: Spektrum;* [16]turtle – *Schildkröte;* [17]breed – *sich fortpflanzen, brüten*; [18]hatch – *schlüpfen*; [19]declare – *erklären, verkünden;* [20]World Heritage Site – *Weltkulturerbe;* [21]flight – *Flug*; [22]balance – *Gleichgewicht*; [23]disturb – *stören;* [24]increasing – *steigend, zunehmend;* [25]due to – *wegen*; [26]duty – *Pflicht*

TB 12 p. 20

3 The Flying Doctor

a) The RFDS is the Royal Flying Doctor Service in Australia. The organisation helps people during emergencies. RFDS pilots sometimes have to battle heavy rain, bushfires and strong winds to get patients to hospital.

You and your mum read what a woman who became a mother for the first time writes about the RFDS and how they helped in an emergency (page 15). Your mum doesn't understand English very well so you have to help out.
Answer her questions in German:

1. Wer war in den Notfall verwickelt?
2. Was genau ist passiert?
3. Wann und wo ist es passiert?
4. Warum war der Einsatz des RFDS erschwert?

b) Choose:

- Look at the notes about the RFDS. Then write a text about the organisation.

- one of the largest aeromedical organisations in the world
- healthcare to people who cannot go to a hospital (Outback)
- founder Reverend John Flynn (1928)
- help in emergencies
- 24 hours a day, 7 days a week
- 79 planes, 23 bases, 1,500 employess
- more than 1,000 patient contacts a day
- about 28,000,000 km's flown a year
- financed through donations (charity)

- Write down the story of Sophie's birth[1] from the pilot's point of view.
- Write down the story of Sophie's birth from the RFD nurse's point of view.

Mercy flight[2] through the storm

Posted by Claire, from Albany, WA – 9 minutes ago

In the days leading up to the arrival of my first child Sophie in 2008, my husband and I were excited, nervous and looking forward to meeting our little one. But on a night in November, as a huge storm raged[3] outside our Albany home, I realized something wasn't right. At four days overdue[4], Sophie had suddenly stopped moving. Within two hours I was in the hospital operating theatre under anesthetic while doctors fought to get Sophie out in time to save her life.

When I woke, my husband told me that Sophie had been tangled in the umbilical cord[5], which had been wrapped six times around her legs, cutting off her oxygen[6] supply. She was born not breathing and without a heartbeat[7]. Because of her lack[8] of oxygen she was seriously unwell with a type of brain injury.

> **Due to the massive weather storm rolling through at the time, the RFDS wasn't able to land at first. But, they didn't give up. Thanks to the persistence of the crew, Sophie got to Perth about 12 hours after birth.**

The moment she was born, Albany hospital had called the Royal Flying Doctor Service and the pilot battled through a ferocious[9] storm to get to Albany and transport Sophie to Princess Margaret Hospital in Perth for urgent treatment. As a result of the loss of oxygen at birth, Sophie required hypothermic treatment[10] that is most effective if administered within six hours. Albany Hospital did an amazing job of starting the process in time, but the clock was ticking.

I didn't know when I would get to see my baby again, but next day the RFDS came to the rescue and picked me up. Not even the combination of major abdominal surgery[11], a chronic fear of flying, a small plane and a whole lot of bad weather could stop me rushing to my child, who was in the Neonatal Intensive Care Unit[12]. Throughout the flight, the RFDS nurse cared for me and two other patients, and we managed to laugh as the pilot joked about practicing for the Red Bull Air Race.

That the RFDS was able to fly me up from Albany to Perth the day after Sophie's birth, so that I could be by her side while her life was still in the balance[13], was one of the most compassionate[14] and meaningful things anyone has ever done for me.

Sophie received treatment for her brain injury in the intensive care unit at Princess Margaret hospital and spent 26 days there. Thankfully, despite a very poor initial[15] prognosis and two years of various therapies, she has made a complete recovery[16], partly because of the prompt treatment she received at birth.

She's now in Year One at school, is a very loving big sister, and is thriving in every respect. Your help during that time will always mean so much to us.

Read more posts

[1]birth – *Geburt*; [2]mercy flight – *Rettungsflug*; [3]rage – *toben, wüten*; [4]overdue – *überfällig*; [5]umbilical cord – *Nabelschnur;* [6]oxygen – *Sauerstoff;* [7]heartbeat – *Herzschlag*; [8]lack – *Mangel*; [9]ferocious – *wild*; [10]hypothermic treatment – *Kältebehandlung;* [11]abdominal surgery – *Bauchoperation;* [12]Neonatal Intensive Care Unit – *Neugeborenenintensivstation;* [13]in the balance – *in der Schwebe, auf der Kippe*; [14]compassionate – *mitfühlend*; [15]initial – *anfänglich;* [16]make a recovery – *gesund werden, sich erholen*

TB PP p.25

4 Aboriginal Australians

a) Look at the pictures. What do you already know about Aboriginal Australians?
b) Read the online article about Aboriginal Australians.
What do you find interesting? Take notes.
c) What does the text say about "terra nullius[1]"? Explain in your own words.
d) Write a short text about the problems Aboriginal Australians face today.

Aboriginal peoples

There are about 500 different Aboriginal peoples in Australia, each with their own language and territory and usually made up of a large number of separate clans.

Archaeologists believe that the Aboriginals first came to the Australian continent around 45,000 years ago. Aboriginals themselves, however, trace their creation back to the Dreamtime, an era long past when the earth was first formed. One Aboriginal man explained it thus: *'By Dreaming we mean the belief[2] that long ago these creatures started human society, they made all natural things and put them in a special place. These Dreaming creatures were connected to special places and special roads or tracks or paths. In many places the great creatures changed themselves into sites[3] where their spirits stayed. Aboriginals have a special connection with everything that is natural. Aboriginals see themselves as part of nature ... All things on earth we see as part human. It is true that people who belong to a particular[4] area are really part of that area and if that area is destroyed they are also destroyed.'*
Aboriginals' land was invaded[5] from the end of the 18th century onwards, with catastrophic consequences for them.

How do they live?
Before the invasion, Aboriginal people lived throughout Australia, although the highest population density was along the coast. Here, people seem to have moved seasonally between permanent settlements near the sea and others at the headwaters of the coast rivers. Evidence suggests that these communities managed their environment carefully to ensure a steady supply of food, bringing wild yams into gardens which they irrigated, for example, or building artificial dykes to extend the range of eels. Those Aboriginal tribes who lived inland[6] in the bush and the desert lived by hunting and gathering[7], burning the undergrowth[8] to encourage[9] the growth of plants favoured by the game[10] they hunted. They were experts in seeking out water.

Today more than half of all Aboriginals live in towns, often on the outskirts[11] in terrible conditions. Many others work as labourers on cattle ranches that have taken over their land. Many, particularly in the northern half of the continent, have managed to cling on to their land and still hunt and gather 'bush tucker'.

What problems do they face?

Ever since the British first invaded, Aboriginal peoples have had their land stolen from them or destroyed. Until 1992, when it was finally overturned[12], the legal principle governing British and then Australian law regarding Aboriginal land was that of 'terra nullius' – that the land was empty before the British arrived, belonged to no-one, and could legitimately be taken over. Most has still to be returned today, and the loss[13] of their land has had a devastating social and physical impact[14] on Aboriginal peoples. The initial invasions also sparked huge waves of disease that killed thousands – many others were massacred. In just over one hundred years from the first invasion of their land, their numbers were reduced from up to an estimated one million to only 60,000.

During much of the 20th century, outright killings were replaced with a policy of removing Aboriginal children from their parents and giving them to white families or placing them in mission schools, to eradicate[15] traces of Aboriginal culture and language. Today they still face racist attitudes, and there are periodic incidents of violence[16] towards them, particularly affecting those in police custody. Their generally poor living conditions mean that Aboriginal people have a far higher infant mortality rate[17] and suicide rate and a lower life expectancy than the rest of the population, and they make up a disproportionate section of the prison population. A landmark High Court judgment in 1992, known as the Mabo case after the lead plaintiff[18], threw out the racist 'terra nullius' principle on which Australian legal attitudes to Aboriginal land rights had been based. The decision recognized for the first time the existence of Aboriginal 'native title' over large parts of rural Australia. Many Aboriginal groups, such as the Martu of western Australia, have used the ruling to have their ownership of their ancestral[19] lands recognized in law. Others, however, have failed to overcome the many legal hurdles[20] placed in their way by the government's land rights legislation.

[1]terra nullius – *Niemandsland*; [2]belief – *Glaube*; [3]site – *Ort*; [4]particular – *bestimmte(r, s)*; [5]invade – *einmarschieren, überfallen;* [6]inland – *im Landesinneren;* [7]gathering – *Sammeln*; [8]undergrowth – *Unterholz*; [9]encourage – *ermutigen, ermuntern*; [10]game – *Wild*; [11]outskirts – *Stadtrand;* [12]overturn – *umkippen, umstürzen;* [13]loss – *Verlust*; [14]impact – *Auswirkung(en), Einfluss*; [15]eradicate – *ausrotten;* [16]violence – *Gewalt(tätigkeit);* [17]infant mortality rate – *Kindersterblichkeitsrate*; [18]plaintiff – *Kläger(in);* [19]ancestral – *Ahnen-, Vorfahren-;* [20]hurdle – *Hürde, Hindernis*

TB 2.1 p. 42

5 Follow the rabbit-proof fence

The book "Follow the rabbit-proof fence" by Doris Pilkington is the true story of three Aboriginal girls who were taken away from their families by the government. They are forced to go to school and train as servants for White families. They want to go home to their families and follow the rabbit-proof fence for over 2000 km to find their way home.

a) Read the extracts from the novel. Constable Riggs, a White policeman in charge of Aboriginal affairs, is taking the sisters Molly and Daisy and her cousin Gracie away from their home.

b) What can you find out about Constable Riggs?
Take notes and try to figure out what kind of person he is.

The three girls were not used to rising before dawn[1] so they settled down in the car and fell asleep. When they opened their eyes they realized that they had slept longer than they expected. They had passed through Ethel Greek and Roy Hills stations and were on the main road to Nullagine, which was an unsealed dirt track, full of potholes[2] and fine red bull dust that seemed to fill the car. They were so exhausted they couldn't cry anymore and they spoke only in whispers[3] and sign language.

Except for a curt[4], "You girls awright back there!" the policeman didn't speak to them or tell the girls where he was taking them. All they knew was they were going to the settlement to go to school. The rain clouds were gathering[5] and by the time they reached the bend where large grey boulders[6] loomed on either side of the road, the sky was black with rain clouds. Riggs glanced up at the dark clouds, while his passengers in the back seat sat silently watching the landscape change as they passed through it. They paid no attention to the beautiful scenery[7] or the long shadows of the tall river gums. Their interest was aroused[8] only when they saw animals such as kangaroos, emus, horses and camels. Otherwise, they sat quite still until one nudged[9] the other to look at something they passed by. In his role as a Protector of the Aborigines, Constable Riggs had been on the move for over a week and would have completed the round trip when he arrived at the Marble Bar. Except for a brief pause at stations along the way they spent most of the day driving. At 2 o'clock they arrived at Marble Bar hospital where Riggs admitted the sick women, then he handed Molly, Gracie and Daisy to Constable Melrose for removal[10] south. Constable Riggs returned to Nullagine at 5pm the same day. With great relief and satisfaction he notified the Chief Protector of Aborigines in Perth by telegram. "All half-castes[11] and sick natives transported Bar train tomorrow report earliest. Riggs Const." 21 July 1931. It was late afternoon when the party reached Marble Bar. When they arrived, Constable Melrose handed Molly, Gracie and Daisy over to his wife as he had to visit the local Aboriginal camp to attend to a young girl who was sick and had to be taken into the Marble Bar hospital.

"Feed them an early supper and I'll lock them up[12] in the empty cells," Melrose told his wife. "I want a good night's sleep tonight." And so while Mimi-Ali and Nellie were resting at the Marble Bar hospital, Molly, Gracie and Daisy spent the next few days at the Marble Bar police station under the supervision[13] of Constable Melrose.

c) Why did Molly decide to leave Marble Bar? What do you think?
d) The girls' way back home was not only long but also dangerous. What dangers can you imagine?

[...]
It was still dark, wet and cold on that morning in August 1931 when the girls were awakened at 5.30. The little ones protested loudly and strongly at being forced to rise at that ungodly hour to leave their warm beds. Molly got up reluctantly[14] and walked out onto the verandah, peeped[15] through the lattice and smiled secretly to herself. Gracie and Daisy joined her but they did not care for the grey, dismal day and said so in no uncertain terms.
The girls waited for Martha and the others to join them, then they made their way through the slushy[16] mud near the stone wall of the staff quarters to the dining room. After a breakfast of weevily porridge, bread and tea, they returned to the dormitory[17] to wait for the school bell. Molly had decided the night before that she and her two sisters were not staying here. She had no desire to live in this strange place amongst people she didn't know. Anyway, she was too big to go to school, they had no right to bring her here.
[...]
It was too early for school, so most of the smaller girls slipped back into bed. Molly, Gracie and Daisy did the same thing but they squashed[18] into the one bed with two girls at the head and Molly at the end.
Molly finished combing her light brown hair and lay watching the movements of the others around her. At the other end of the bed Daisy and Gracie were whispering quietly to each other. Daisy, aged nine, had the same coloured hair and texture as her elder sister, while Gracie had straight, black hair that hung down to her shoulders. It was very apparent that the three girls had inherited[19] features from their white fathers. The only obvious Aboriginal characteristics were their dark brown eyes and their ability to control their facial expressions, so that when they reached maturity[20] they would develop the look of a quiet, dignified Aboriginal woman from the Pilbara region.
[...]
As soon as the other girls left the dormitory, Molly beckoned[21] her two sisters to come closer to her, then she whispered urgently, "We're not going to school, so grab your bags. We're not staying here." Daisy and Gracie were stunned and stood staring at her.
"What did you say?" said Gracie.
"I said, we're not staying here at the settlement, because we're going home to Jigalong."
Gracie and Daisy weren't sure whether they were hearing correctly or not.
"Move quickly," Molly ordered her sisters. She wanted to be miles away before their absence[22] was discovered. Time was of the essence.
Her two young sisters faced each other, both looking very scared and confused. Daisy turned to Molly and said nervously, "We're frightened Dgudu. How are we going to find our way back home to Jigalong? It's a long way from home."
Molly leaned against the wall and said confidently, "I know it's a long way to go but it's easy. We'll find the rabbit-proof fence and follow that all the way home."

[1]dawn – *Morgendämmerung*; [2]pothole – *Schlagloch*; [3]speak in whispers – *flüstern*; [4]curt – *schroff, barsch*; [5]gather – *hier: sich zusammenziehen*; [6]boulder – *Felsbrocken*; [7]scenery – *Landschaft*; [8]arouse – *erwecken, erregen*; [9]nudge – *stoßen, schubsen*; [10]removal – *Umzug*; [11]half-caste – *Mischling, Halbblut*; [12]lock sb up – *jdn einsperren*; [13]supervision – *Beaufsichtigung*; [14]reluctant – *widerwillig*; [15]peep – *spähen*; [16]slushy – *matschig*; [17]dormitory – *Schlafsaal*; [18]squash – *sich zwängen*; [19]inherit – *erben*; [20]maturity – *Reife, Erwachsensein*; [21]beckon – *sein Zeichen geben*; [22]absence – *Abwesenheit, Fehlen*

TB 2 p. 46

1 Why New Zealand?

a) Why do you think New Zealand is the birthplace of so many extreme sports? Note down your ideas.

b) Read the article from a sports magazine. What reasons does the author mention? Compare them to your ideas and complete your list.

New Zealand – a thrillseeker[1]'s playground

If you think about extreme sports, you might think about danger and fun combined into one. That is exactly the idea: You do something that is extremely dangerous, perhaps even life-threatening, and the adrenaline rush[2] we get from it makes it so thrilling that it overpowers[3] the fear[4] of danger. Of course, not everybody enjoys extreme sports but people who do will probably make their way to a certain country at some point in their lives: New Zealand. New Zealand is home to many extreme sports, such as bungee jumping, zorbing and jet boating. But why is it that New Zealand has become a thrillseeker's playground and not any other country? Although the answer isn't so straightforward[5], I've had time to sit down and think about it. The first obvious reason could be the diverse landscape. You have rugged[6] mountains and vast[7] plains[8], but also long coastlines, glaciers and volcanoes. The landscape is so diverse that there are always lots of new things to try out.

Some people look to the history and culture of New Zealand to find an answer. Consider all the people who have come to New Zealand, such as the Maori who first arrived in New Zealand 1,000 years ago, to Abel Tasman and James Cook from Europe. They were all adventurers. Some say that the bungee is a modern version of a ritual from Pentecost Island in the South Pacific nation of Vanuatu. This ritual involved[9] young men who tied[10] vines[11] around their ankles and then jumped off big towers. It was a symbol to show that they were becoming men. Perhaps history and culture both play a role when it comes to extreme sports in New Zealand.

A final reason why people do extreme sports in New Zealand is insurance[12]. Let's take the US, for example. In the US, it is very easy to be sued[13] for something you did wrong. People are very careful. In New Zealand, insurance works differently. The ACC – Accident Compensation[14] Corporation – covers residents and tourists. The insurance cover[15] is interesting because fault is never the issue. In other words, you can't blame[16]

[1]thrillseeker – *der/die Abenteuerlustige*; [2]rush – *hier: Rausch*; [3]overpower – *überwältigen*; [4]fear – *Angst, Furcht*; [5]straightforward – *direkt, einfach;* [6]rugged – *zerklüftet;* [7]vast – *gewaltig, weit*; [8]plains – *Ebene, Flachland*; [9]involve – *beinhalten, umfassen*; [10]tie – *binden*; [11]vine – *Liane;* [12]insurance – *Versicherung;* [13]sue – *verklagen*; [14]compensation – *Schadenersatz*; [15]insurance cover – *Versicherungsschutz;* [16]blame – *die Schuld geben, verantwortlich machen*

somebody for doing something. For example, if you fall off your rented bike because you get a flat tyre, you get paid. It doesn't matter if it was your fault (you cycled carelessly over lots of sharp nails) or the fault of the bike rental company (the wheels were really old and already damaged). Because they don't have to fear expensive lawsuits[17], tour operators in New Zealand are able to create risky and extreme adventure scenarios for tourists to try out.

So, why am I writing about all of this? I would call myself an adventurer, which is why I went to New Zealand to see what all the fuss[18] is about with extreme sports. First I tried jet boating. It was invented by a Kiwi farmer called Sir William Hamilton. He wanted a quick and easy way to travel up rocky rivers, so in 1954 he came up with the idea of jet boating. I would say jet boating was fun, but a little too calm for my taste. But that is what makes it so special – it is accessible[19] to everyone (as long as[20] you don't mind getting very wet!).

Another sport I tried was zorbing. In very simple words: This is where you enter a giant, inflatable sphere and roll down a hill. This sport was first started in 1994 on the North Island of New Zealand. The initial idea was to be able to walk on water when you are playing on the beach. The big problem: It is difficult to control where you are going! So the idea was changed to rolling down a big hill instead.

The third and final extreme sport I tried in New Zealand was bungee jumping. Do you know the story behind the ritual from Pentecost Island? According to the legend, a woman tried to run away from her abusive[21] husband. She tied vines around her legs and jumped down from a tree. Her husband tried to chase her and jumped off the tree, too. But he didn't notice the vines. The woman landed safely on the ground and the man died. From that day on, men started to practice jumping with vines so that women could never outsmart[22] them again.

Modern bungee jumping first started in 1979, but not in New Zealand – in Bristol, UK. Members of the Oxford Dangerous Sports Club performed a few jumps from Clifton Bridge. They were put into prison for a few days (it was illegal after all), but the popularity[23] of bungee jumping started spreading around the world. In 1989, the first commercial[24] bungee jumping site was opened by A. J. Hackett in Queensland, New Zealand.

My heart was racing when I started to get ready for my bungee jump. The idea behind

[17]lawsuit – *Klage, Gerichtsverfahren*; [18]fuss – *(übertriebene) Aufregung*; [19]accessible – *(leicht) erreichbar, zugänglich*; [20]as long as – *sofern, solange*; [21]abusive – *misshandelnd*; [22]outsmart – *austricksen;* [23]popularity – *Beliebtheit, Popularität*; [24]commercial – *kommerziell, profitorientiert*

it is very simple. You put on two harnesses[25]. One is attached to your ankle and another to your body. These harnesses are attached to a large bungee cord[26]. And then, you jump! What a thrill it was! But I think it is something that is once in a lifetime[27]. I definitely don't need to do it again …

You can go bungee jumping in many places in New Zealand. I went at Kawarau Bridge near Queenstown. You could also try the biggest bungee jump in New Zealand (and third biggest in the world): The Nevis. I love an adventure, but that would have been too much for me (the fall is three times higher than the Statue of Liberty!). Estimates[28] show that around 150,000 people go bungee jumping in New Zealand every year (which is a lot when you consider that just under three million people visit New Zealand every year).

Do you think you could be one of those 150,000 people next year?

[25]harness – *Gurtzeug;* [26]bungee cord – *Gurt (mit Haken)*; [27]once in a lifetime – *einmalig, einmal im Leben*; [28]estimate – *Schätzung*

c) The author has tried some extreme sports. If you had the chance to fly to New Zealand, which of the mentioned sports would you try? Why? Why not? Write it down.

TB 2 p. 46

2 Extreme sports

Look at the article about extreme sports on pages 20 to 22 again.
What do you learn about the different sports?
Choose one and take notes. Use the Internet to find out more information about the extreme sport. Then write a short text about it.
Think about

- its roots
- people involved in the invention
- how you do it
- where you can do it
- what equipment you need
- how many people do it.

3 Taking sports to the extreme

TB 9 p. 50

a) Read the online article. What is it about? Summarise it in three to four sentences.

b) Answer the questions.

1. How are injuries seen that incurred in activities like riding a bike or running? How are injuries seen that result from extreme sports?
2. What does 26-year-old Jody say about what she experiences when she goes river surfing?
3. Why is fear an essential element in extreme sports?
4. What reasons for doing extreme sports are mentioned?
5. How can hazards in extreme sports be minimized?

c) What do you think about extreme sports? Explain your opinion in about five sentences.

BY JANE E. BRODY AUGUST 15

Mountain biking, helicopter skiing, river surfing, BASE jumping, waterfall kayaking, ice climbing and other extreme sports that put participants at risk[1] of serious injury, even death, grow annually[2] in popularity.

I know what you're thinking, I thought it too: Why would anyone pursue[3] activities so dangerous that you must sign a waiver[4] absolving[5] the organizers of all responsibility[6] for a catastrophic accident? One small slip, a brief lapse of attention, and you're history.

The traditional public perception[7] is that "extreme sports participation is an unhealthy, pathological[8] need for uncertainty[9], thrills and excitement," Eric Brymer, an exercise specialist, wrote in 2010 (...).

But is it really just about chasing an adrenaline rush? And are these action sports as dangerous to devoted[10] participants[11] as they seem on television and in YouTube videos? (...)

There are no reliable statistics to inform a potential participant of the risks of any sport, even everyday activities school children and amateur and professional athletes engage in[12], like soccer, skateboarding, basketball and football. While individual injuries and deaths are

[1]put at risk – *gefährden, in Gefahr bringen*; [2]annual – *jährlich*; [3]pursue – *verfolgen*; [4]waiver – *Erlass, Verzichtserklärung*; [5]absolve – *freisprechen, entlassen*; [6]responsibility – *Verantwortung*; [7]perception – *Wahrnehmung*; [8]pathological – *krankhaft*; [9]uncertainty – *Ungewissheit, Unsicherheit*; [10]devoted – *begeistert*; [11]participant – *Teilnehmer/in*; [12]engage in – *sich beteiligen an*

well publicized[13], there are no data to show how likely[14] these are. Furthermore, Jamie F. Burr of the University of Prince Edward Island and colleagues wrote in Canadian Family Physician[15], the public perception of risk is distorted[16]: "Risk-taking is inherently human[17] and can be an important factor in personal development. Injuries incurred[18] while engaging in more traditional physical activities are regarded as 'unfortunate[19] accidents,' while injuries resulting from participation in adventure sports are viewed as 'foreseeable[20] and foolhardy[21].'"

Second, the motivations offered by extreme sports participants for why they are so willing to assume[22] the risks involved are not what you might expect. Adventure sports are not "an outlet for 'crazy' individuals with an unhealthy relationship to fear, who are pathological in their search for risk or living out a death wish," Dr. Brymer and his colleague at Queensland University, Robert Schweitzer, wrote. (...)

A study by John H. Kerr, a kinesiologist at the University of British Columbia, and Susan Houge Mackenzie, a movement specialist then at the University of Idaho, quoted a 26-year-old river surfer identified only as Jody, who said, "You're just stoked[23]." Then she added, "It's not just your adrenaline. It's a sense of achievement[24]. You set out to do something and you've done it — it's everything leading up to it, the skills that you have or the hard work that you've done."

Nor is it that extreme sports participants lack[25] fear. "Fear is an essential element to their survival," Dr. Brymer and Dr. Schweitzer explained. In interviews with extreme athletes, they and other researchers have learned that participants consider fear "a healthy, productive experience," prompting[26] them to take appropriate precautions[27] that enhance the chances of surviving uninjured[28].

As one solo rope-free mountain climber told the researchers, "If I panic, I'm lost, dead." He learned to thwart[29] panic and instead stay relaxed and focused, maintaining clarity and good judgment that help to protect him.

Also important, a 30-year-old BASE jumper identified as "TB" told Dr. Brymer, is to "learn everything possible about the sport; learn about weather conditions, learn about wind, learn about what wind does in and around buildings and structures and cliffs, etc., so you know what you can do and what you can't do."

[13]publicize – *bekanntmachen, Werbung machen für*; [14]likely – *wahrscheinlich*; [15]Canadian Family Physician – *medizinische Zeitschrift*; [16]distorted – *verzerrt*; [17]human – *menschlich;* [18]incur – *entstehen, hervorrufen;* [19]unfortunate – *unglücklich, bedauerlich*; [20]forseeable – *vorhersehbar*; [21]foolhardy – *waghalsig*; [22]assume – *annehmen, eingehen*; [23]stoked – *aufgeregt;* [24]achievement – *Leistung, Errungenschaft;* [25]lack – *nicht haben, fehlen*; [26]prompt – *veranlassen*; [27]take precautions – *Vorsichtsmaßnahmen treffen;* [28]uninjured – *unverletzt;* [29]thwart – *hier: verhindern*

Through interviews with many regular extreme sports participants, researchers have found that the emotional high becomes less and less important with time. As participants continue to pursue the activities, other motives and perceived[30] benefits[31] to health and well-being take precedence[32].

Mr. Kerr and Dr. Mackenzie reported that participants experienced such benefits as feeling strong, healthy and fit; connecting with nature and being more in touch with one's surroundings; gaining self-confidence[33]; and becoming self-sufficient[34].

Overcoming fear is a near-universal goal for participants, the Australian researchers wrote. A young woman BASE jumper they interviewed described fear as a gateway to transcendence, calling her sport the "ultimate metaphor for jumping into life rather than standing on the edge[35] quivering."

Devoted extreme sport participants regard safety as their highest priority. They learn the skills needed for their chosen sport, they train to become sufficiently expert at it and to know how to judge[36] the extent[37] of their ability, said Dr. Vani Sabesan, an orthopedic surgeon at Western Michigan University School of Medicine.

"Someone with medical expertise[38] should be present to make sure you have the right protective gear[39] and to rescue you if something goes wrong," she said.

(...)

Dr. McGowen emphasized the importance of having an athletic trainer present at all organized activities — school and youth leagues as well as amateur and professional games, who can enhance safety[40] through proper nutrition[41], well-maintained equipment and good coaching, as well as properly care for an injured athlete.

Such guidance is especially important for people planning to participate in an extreme sport. "People are terrible judges of risk," David O. Horton, a professor of law at the University of California, Davis, told me. "They don't understand the language of the contracts[42] they sign saying that they have no legal rights if something should go wrong. Organizers don't have to spell out all the risks for the contract to be enforceable."

His advice: "Be as cleareyed[43] as you can be about what can possibly go wrong — ask questions, do research about potential downsides, and don't try anything you're not capable of or properly equipped to do."

[30]perceived – *wahrgenommen, empfunden*; [31]benefit – *Vorteil, Nutzen*; [32]take precedence – *Vorrang haben*; [33]self-confidence – *Selbstvertrauen*; [34]self-sufficient – *unabhängig;* [35]edge – *Rand, hier: Ufer;* [36]judge – *(be)urteilen, entscheiden*; [37]extent – *Ausmaß, Umfang*; [38]expertise – *Fachkenntnis, Kompetenz*; [39]gear – *Ausrüstung*; [40]enhance saftey – *Sicherheit erhöhen;* [41]nutrition – *Ernährung;* [42]contract – *Vertrag*; [43]cleareyed – *scharfsichtig*

TB 4 p.55

4 The legend of New Zealand

a) There are lots of myths and legends in the Maori culture. One of them is about the creation of New Zealand. Read the website on page 27 about how New Zealand was created according to the legend of Maui and the magic fishhook[1].

b) Your grandma doesn't understand English very well but is really interested in New Zealand. Answer her questions.

1. Was steht da über Maui? Wer war das?
2. Ich verstehe, dass Maui mit seinen Brüdern fischen war. Was hat das mit Neuseeland zu tun?
3. Wie erklärt die Legende die Täler, Berge und Seen auf der Nordinsel?
4. Was wird über die Südinsel gesagt?

[1]fishhook – *Angelhaken*

TB 4 p.55

5 Maui and the magic fishhook

a) Look at the information on page 27 again.
Then write the legend of Maui and the magic fishhook in your own words.
You can make a comic with pictures and speech bubbles[1], too.

b) Do you know a legend of YOUR area? Write it down.

[1]speech bubble – *Sprechblase*

Home | Facts about New Zealand | History | The Legend of New Zealand

Maori legend says New Zealand was fished from the sea by the daring[1] demigod[2] Māui. According to Maori and Polynesian myths and legends, Māui was the gifted and clever demigod who won the affection[3] of his supernatural parents after a miraculous[4] birth and upbringing[5]. He was bold and sharp-witted[6] and taught useful arts to mankind[7], although he was not always liked. He tamed[8] the sun and brought fire to the world, but one of his most famous feats[9] was the creation of the islands we know today as Aotearoa, New Zealand.

Maori believe that one-night Māui's four brothers planned to go fishing and leave him behind. Overhearing their plans and not wanting to be left out, Māui hid under the floorboards[10] of his brother's canoe and waited until they were far away from the shore before revealing himself. He had carved[11] a magic fishhook from an ancestors' jawbone[12] and he cast[13] it deep into the sea, chanting powerful words.

Soon, Māui realised he had caught something. Something huge! With the help of his brothers, the catch was hurled to the surface[14] of the water. Much to their surprise, the fish they had caught was in fact a huge piece of land and they were delighted to find that they had discovered 'Te Ika a Māui' (Māui's fish), which we know today as the North Island.

Before Māui had time to thank Tangaroa (the god of the sea) for the gift of this land, Māui's brothers began carving out pieces of the huge fish, creating the many valleys, mountains, and lakes that you see today on the North Island.

'Te Waka a Māui' (Māui's canoe) or what we know now as the South Island is said to be the waka or canoe that Māui and his brothers fished from. It's believed that the Kaikōura Peninsula[15] on the east coast of the South Island is the place where the seat of the canoe was situated, where Māui stood to haul in[16] his giant catch.

Stewart Island-Rakiura is believed to be the anchor[17] from the canoe and is named 'Te Punga a Māui' (Māui's anchor stone).

Read more legends

[1]daring – *kühn, wagemutig*; [2]demigod – *Halbgott*; [3]affection – *Zuneigung, Liebe*; [4]miraculous – *wunderbar*; [5]upbringing – *Erziehung*; [6]sharp-witted – *scharfsinnig*; [7]mankind – *Menschheit*; [8]tame – *zähmen*; [9]feat – *Heldentat*; [10]floorboard – *Diele(nbrett)*; [11]carve – *schnitzen, einritzen*; [12]jawbone – *Kieferknochen*; [13]cast – *(aus)werfen*; [14]surface – *Oberfläche*; [15]peninsula – *Halbinsel*; [16]haul in – *sich schnappen*; [17]anchor – *Anker*

TB 8 p.58

6 Aotearoa or New Zealand?

a) Read the article. What is it about? Summarise it in two sentences.

b) Answer the questions.
1. Why did 70,000 people sign the petition mentioned in the article?
2. What would the problem be with a referendum for the issue?
3. Ngarewa-Packer says a name change is "not a matter[1] of if, but when". What does she mean?

c) Should the country's name be changed? Why? Why not? Write down your opinion.

Aotearoa or New Zealand: has the moment come to change the country's name?

It's not the first push[2] to adopt[3] the te reo Māori name, but a petition signed by 70,000 people has given it fresh momentum

What's in a name? A lot, when it comes to a nation's identity. Recognition[4] is growing within Aotearoa New Zealand over the importance of te reo Māori (Māori language), and with it a renewed push to change the country's official name – this time backed[5] by a petition[6] with 70,000 signatures[7].
The petition (…) was launched by the Māori party[8] in September 2021 and has recently been submitted to parliament for consideration[9].
It calls on the government to[10] change New Zealand's official name to Aotearoa (pronounced ow-tear-roh-ah), a te reo Māori name for the country, and to "identify and officially restore[11] the original te reo Māori names for all towns, cities and places right across the country" over the next five years, completing the process by[12] 2026. (…)

Where did the name New Zealand come from?
As with all colonised countries, naming played an important role in staking a claim[13] on an area of land and acting as a nostalgic connection to home. Sometimes, names were given due to mistaken[14] geography, as was the case with Abel Tasman, who first sighted the already inhabited shores in 1642. He named the land Staten Land because he believed the land was connected to Isla de los Estados (Staten Island), now modern Argentina.
Sometime later a cartographer[15] from the Dutch East India Company[16] bestowed[17] the name Nieuw Zeeland after the coastal province Zeeland in the Netherlands. The Dutch had very little to do with the country from then on, and when James Cook arrived in 1769 he anglicised the name to New Zealand.

Where does the name Aotearoa come from?
According to a group of University of Waikato academics writing in The Conversation, the precise origin[18] of the name – which is commonly translated to "long white cloud" or "long bright world" – is not known.
There are indications[19] it has been in use for a long time. Sir George Grey used Aotearoa in

[1]matter – *Angelegenheit, Sache*; [2]push – *Anstoß*; [3]adopt – *annehmen, übernehmen*; [4]recognition – *hier: Anerkennung*; [5]backed – *unterlegt*; [6]petition – *Petition, Bittschrift*; [7]signature – *Unterschrift*; [8]party – *Partei*; [9]submit for consideration – *einreichen, vorlegen*; [10]call on sb to do sth – *jdn auffordern, etw zu tun*; [11]restore – *wiederherstellen*; [12]by – *hier: bis*; [13]stake a claim – *Anspruch anmelden*; [14]mistaken – *irrtümlich, falsch*; [15]cartographer – *Kartograph/in*; [16]Dutch East India Company – *Niederländische Ostindien-Kompanie, Zusammenschluss niederländischer Kaufmannskompanien*; [17]bestow – *verleihen*; [18]origin – *Ursprung, Herkunft*; [19]indication – *Hinweis*

his writing in 1855 and 1857, it is referenced in Māori language newspapers, and the Māori Legal Corpus – a digitised[20] collection of thousands of pages of legal texts in te reo Māori spanning[21] 1829 to 2009 – mentions Aotearoa 2,748 times.

But not all Māori iwi (tribes) have the same connection to the name. The southern most iwi, Ngāi Tahu, has warned against rushing into a name change that may overlook the South Island. Kaumatua (elder[22]) Edward Ellison told RNZ[23] a more commonly used title in the south was Aotearoa me Te Waipounamu, which encompassed[24] both major land masses.

How successful is the petition likely[25] to be?

The petition gathered[26] just over 70,000 signatures, which co-leader Debbie Ngarewa-Packer said was "really telling that people are hungry for change". (…) The party was "over the moon[27]" with the level of public support for a name change.

The petition is now being considered by the petitions committee[28]. However, should it progress[29] further, it is likely to hit an impasse[30], with the National party and right-wing party ACT[31] against a change. National's leader, Christopher Luxon, has suggested the issue should be decided by a referendum[32], but told 1 News there was unlikely to be widespread support. "I don't think there's much appetite for it at all."

Ngarewa-Packer said a referendum would be unfair to Māori because they represent just 17% of the population, an imbalance[33] caused by colonisation.

What is the public mood?

A name change would not require[34] a huge leap of imagination for some – the name is increasingly being used by members of the public, within media, businesses and government and it features on New Zealand's passport.

Prime minister Jacinda Ardern has said she uses both interchangeably[35] and hopes the country will follow suit, but has not committed to an official name change. "Whether or not we change it in law I don't think changes the fact New Zealanders do increasingly refer to Aotearoa, and I think that's a transition that has been welcomed."

But a poll[36] late last year shows the majority of New Zealanders may not be ready yet. Just over half of the respondents (58%) said they wanted to stick with the status quo, but the bloc of respondents who wanted Aotearoa somewhere in the name – be it solely (9%) or a combination of Aotearoa New Zealand (31%) was sizeable[37].

If the petition fails, what will that mean for future attempts[38]?

Ngarewa-Packer says a name change is "not a matter of if, but when". "We're continually pushing and reminding our nation to remember that it is one thing to make te reo Māori our official language, but it is another thing to commit to bringing it to life and the stories and histories attached."

The Māori party has a lot of confidence[39] in younger generations, Ngarewa-Packer said. "There is more appetite for change, there is more maturing[40] over the need to have a conversation about who we are and how we identify as a nation."

[20]digitised – *digitalisiert*; [21]span – *umfassen*; [22]elder – *Stammesälteste(r)*; [23]RNZ – *Radio New Zealand*; [24]encompass – *umfassen;* [25]likely – *wahrscheinlich;* [26]gather – *sammeln*; [27]over the moon – *überglücklich*; [28]committee – *Ausschuss*; [29]progress – *vorankommen, fortschreiten*; [30]impasse – *Sackgasse;* [31]ACT – *rechts angesiedelte liberale politische Partei;* [32]referendum – *Referendum, Volksabstimmung*; [33]imbalance – *Ungleichgewicht*; [34]require – *benötigen;* [35]interchangeable – *austauschbar;* [36]poll – *Umfrage*; [37]sizeable – *ziemlich groß, beträchtlich;* [38]attempt – *Versuch;* [39]confidence – *Vertrauen, Zuversicht;* [40]mature – *heranreifen, sich weiterentwickeln*

TB 2 p. 77

1 About friendship

a) Read the lyrics of the two songs about friendship on pages 30 and 31.
Summarise the overall message of both of them.
What kind of feelings do the songs evoke?

True friend - Jeannie Lurie

We sign our cards and letters BFF
You've got a million ways to make me laugh[1]
You're looking out for[2] me, you've got my back[3]
It's so good to have you around

You know the secrets I could never tell
And when I'm quiet you break through[4] my shell
Don't feel the need to do a rebel yell[5]
'Cause you keep my feet on the ground

(You're) a true friend
You're here till the end
You pull me aside when something ain't[6] right
Talk with me now and into the night
Till it's alright again
You're a true friend

You don't get angry when I change the plans
Somehow[7] you're never out of[8] second chances
Won't say 'I told you' when I'm wrong again
I'm so lucky that I've found

A true friend
You're here 'til the end
You pull me aside when something ain't right
Talk with me now and into the night
'Til it's alright again

True friends will go to the end of the earth
Till they find the things you need
Friends hang on through the ups and the downs[9]
'Cause they've got someone to believe in

A true friend
You're here 'til the end
You pull me aside when something ain't right
Talk with me now and into the night
No need to pretend[10], you're a

True friend
You're here 'til the end
You pull me aside when somethin' ain't right
Talk with me now and into the night
'Til it's alright again

You're a true friend, you're a true friend
You're a true friend

[1]make sb laugh – *jdn zum Lachen bringen*; [2]look out for sb/sth – *auf jdn/etw achten*; [3]have sb's back – *jdm den Rücken freihalten*; [4]break through – *sich durchdrängen, überwinden*; [5]rebel yell – *(Kampf)schrei;* [6]ain't – *informal: isn't;* [7]somehow – *irgendwie*; [8]be out of sth – *etw nicht mehr haben*; [9]ups and downs – *das Auf und Ab*; [10]pretend – *(sich) etw vormachen*

We're going to be friends - The White Stripes

Fall[1] is here, hear the yell[2]
back to school, ring the bell
brand new shoes, walking blues
climb the fence, books and pens
I can tell that we are gonna be friends
I can tell that we are gonna be friends

Walk with me, Suzy Lee
through the park and by the tree
we will rest upon[3] the ground
and look at all the bugs[4] we found
safely walk to school without a sound
safely walk to school without a sound

Here we are, no one else[5]
we walked to school all by ourselves
there's dirt[6] on our uniforms
from chasing all the ants[7] and worms
we clean up and now it's time to learn
we clean up and now it's time to learn

Numbers, letters, learn to spell
nouns, and books, and show and tell
playtime[8] we will throw the ball
back to class, through the hall
teacher marks our height against the wall
teacher marks our height against the wall

We don't notice any time pass
we don't notice anything
we sit side by side in every class
teacher thinks that I sound funny
but she likes the way you sing

Tonight I'll dream while I'm in bed
when silly thoughts go through my head
about the bugs and alphabet
and when I wake tomorrow I'll bet[9]
that you and I will walk together again
I can tell that we are gonna be friends
Yes I can tell that we are gonna be friends.

[1]fall – *AE: Herbst*; [2]yell – *(Auf)schrei*; [3]upon – *auf*; [4]bug – *Insekt, Krabbeltier*; [5]else – *sonst, anders;* [6]dirt – *Schmutz, Dreck;* [7]ant – *Ameise*; [8]playtime – *Pause, Freizeit*; [9]bet – *wetten*

b) Compare the two songs. Take notes on similarities and differences.

c) Write a text about the two songs and point out what is similar and what is different. Include how old the friends in the songs are, what makes them friends and why they like each other. Prove your ideas with quotes from the lyrics of the two songs.

> The song "True friend" is about two best friends.
> The two teenagers …

d) What kind of attitude do you have towards friendship? Find a song which reflects your ideas. Explain what friendship means to you using quotes from the lyrics of your chosen song.

TB 3 p. 78

2 Cartoons

a) Look at the cartoons. What do they have in common?

"Mom, tell me again about the times you didn't have to tap 'Add' when you made a new friend."

"So – we meet at last."

b) What do the cartoons try to express about friendships and relationships in the modern world? Talk about them with a partner.

c) Do you think modern technology helps or hinders communication? Write a short comment.

TB 3 p. 78

3 Gabe and Benji

a) Read Gabe's story about the friendship with his best friend Benji.

b) Write about the development of their friendship in as much detail as possible. These questions can help you:

1. What was Benji and Gabe's friendship like when they first met?
2. What happened to their friendship when they got older?
3. How did they become friends again?

c) Write the story from Benji's point of view.

> I used to have a friend called Gabe.
> We first met when ...

I first met my friend Benji when we were both six years old. I remember our first conversation; it was about dinosaurs. We talked about dinosaurs a lot back then. Benji and I got on like a house on fire[1] from the moment we met. We both loved dinosaurs and cars and any kind of machine. I was really into[2] computers from an early age as well. Benji didn't like computers so much. He loved to read. When we were kids, those differences didn't matter. When we moved to another school, Benji and I stuck together. We spent our lunch breaks together and shared quite a few[3] lessons. We hung out most days after school as well[4]. I would normally be at Benji's place and his mum would let us have biscuits and sweets. She wasn't very strict[5] at all. Benji even got a game console after a while so we could play games. I think he got it mainly for me. I don't think he ever played when I wasn't there. When we got a bit older though[6], we started to spend less time together. I met new friends, I started going to the computer club and I just didn't want to hang out with Benji that much anymore. I think I was pretty mean to him. I knew he was upset and hurt that I didn't want to spend time with him but he never said anything. By the time we were teenagers we only saw each other in school and most days we didn't talk to each other at all. I noticed Benji had made new friends as well so I didn't feel bad. I said to myself that we had nothing in common anyway. I was very involved in the computer club and I spent all my spare time[7] in front of a screen, gaming. I didn't really do anything else anymore. I went to school, got home and sat down in front of the computer. Actually[8] it was becoming a bit of a problem. I didn't really talk to anyone anymore unless[9] they were in my gaming team. I didn't do my homework and sometimes I didn't go to school either[10]. My parents were getting really worried and I had a lot of arguments with them. But I just wanted to play. One day, a new player joined the game. He was cool. He knew some great stuff about strategy and positioning[11]. He mentioned that he lived in my town as well. We played together for a few months and then a film based on our game came out. My team mates[12] who lived near me, including the new guy, and I made arrangements[13] for a real live meet-up. We wanted to watch the film together. When I got to the cinema, the first person I saw was Benji. I couldn't believe it. He was the new guy and we had been playing together for months. So, Benji and I did have something in common. We started talking again after that. Not just in the game. We texted each other and Benji came up to me at school to chat. It was great. We started meeting up again as well. We went to the mall or to the cinema or just hung out. I started playing less and spending more time with Benji. I think my friendship with Benji helped me to get away from gaming too much. He made me leave the house again and think about something else than computers and games. I still feel really bad about being mean to Benji when we were younger. I'm glad he stuck around and didn't give up on me[14]. I'm sure now that we'll be friends for life and I can count on him when times are tough.

[1]get on like a house on fire – *ausgezeichnet/hervorragend miteinander auskommen*; [2]be into sth – *an etw interessiert sein, auf etw stehen*; [3]quite a few – *ziemlich viele*; [4]as well – *auch*; [5]strict – *streng;* [6]though – *(je)doch;* [7]spare time – *Freizeit*; [8]actually – *hier: tatsächlich*; [9]unless – *außer (wenn);* [10]not either – *auch nicht*; [11]positioning – *Positionierung, Platzierung*; [12]team mate – *Mitspieler/in;* [13]make arrangements – *organisieren, etw abmachen*; [14]give up on sth – *jdn aufgeben, jdn abschreiben*

TB 8 p. 82

4 I was a troll

a) Look at the definition of what an Internet troll is.
Think about when you have come across someone like that.

> **INTERNET TROLL**
>
> An Internet troll, also simply known as a "troll", is a person who purposely posts rude, offensive, or misleading comments online to upset or annoy others. Trolls often want to create arguments rather than engage in meaningful discussions. They do this for attention or amusement, and their behaviour can disrupt online communities. This behaviour can be harmful and it is characterised by a lack of respect for others in online interactions.

b) Read the newspaper article. Why do you think the troll started bullying Emily?
What feelings and emotions did he go through? What should he have done instead?

c) Write a summary of the article.
Make sure you follow the rules for summary writing.

> **Summary**
> 1. Write an opening sentence to introduce the text.
> 2. Use the present tense.
> 3. Use your own words (i.e. find synonyms and paraphrase).
> 4. Use formal language.
> 5. Do not use direct speech.
> 6. Leave out unnecessary details.
> 7. Don't give your opinion.
> 8. Don't analyse the text.

I was a troll

Anonymous[1]

A few years ago when I was in Year 10, a new girl joined my class. She was called Emily and she moved to our town because her mum had got a new job.
She was a very pleasant[2] and quietly confident girl. It soon became clear that her favourite subject was art. Whenever[3] you saw her, she always had her nose in a sketchbook[4] filled with her beautiful artwork[5]. Her unique behaviour made her a perfect target[6] to be bullied by the more popular kids at school. There wasn't any violent[7] bullying – there were just lots of nasty things said to her, and they mimicked[8] her northern accent[9] (she was from Leeds). I once, without really thinking, mimicked

her accent and said something cruel to her. Her eyes filled with tears[10] and her shoulders slumped down in defeat[11].

But I didn't feel regret[12]. I felt a feeling of strength and power – as if I had finally found my place at school.

One day, I was chatting to two of my classmates when one of them came up with the idea to create a fake social media account to troll[13] Emily – anonymously, of course. Feeling excited at the chance to get close to my classmates, I agreed.

And so we created our account. Emily posted her drawings[14] on her social media account, and we began commenting on them, saying how horrible her artwork was and that she should give up on her dreams of becoming a professional artist in the future.

My classmates and I would meet up after school to brainstorm new ways to troll her online. I felt so powerful seeing her become quieter and quieter from a distance. We even started posting rumours[15] about her which weren't true at all but people were quick to believe.

Over the next weeks, Emily started being late for class. One day, she didn't turn up at all. In the evening, I was preparing to send another comment from our fake social media account when I saw she had posted a picture of a wilting[16] flower. As a caption, she had written: "Even the weakest[17] can find strength within."

That's when it hit me. What was I doing?

Emily was a brand new pupil at our school. She had to move to a place where she didn't know anyone, and she clearly chose to get lost[18] in her art because that was the only company she had. She was innocently sharing her artwork with her old friends from her old school on social media, and then we came along and ruined[19] it all.

I started to distance[20] myself from the classmates I had made the fake social media account with. I deleted the account, which made them furious[21] – and so they stopped talking to me. I didn't care though[22]. Over the next few weeks, I started to observe[23] Emily from a distance. She was distraught[24]. You could see how she was holding back the tears every time somebody spoke to her. She looked drained from her attempts to overcome the bullying.

Finally, I plucked up the courage[25] to speak to her, and I tried to support her through the bullying. Soon enough, people got bored of trolling her online and bullying her at school, but I stayed with her as a friend.

Emily started to open up to me and told me about how her father had been an artist. He had passed away when she was five years old, which is why she is so passionate about drawing and painting. The guilt[26] sunk even deeper inside me.

And that guilt still stays with me today.

I never had the guts[27] to tell her that I had been one of the anonymous Internet trolls. I wish that I had never put my own selfish needs, being popular in school, in front of the well-being of others. I will never forgive myself for what I did.

---

[1]anonymous – *anonym*; [2]pleasant – *angenehm*; [3]whenever – *immer wenn, wann (auch) immer*; [4]sketchbook – *Skizzenbuch;* [5]artwork – *Kunstwerk*; [6]target – *Ziel*; [7]violent – *brutal, gewalttätig*; [8]mimic – *nachahmen, nachäffen*; [9]accent – *Akzent*; [10]tear – *Träne*; [11]defeat – *Niederlage*; [12]regret – *Bedauern, Reue*; [13]troll – *trollen, destruktiv und unsachlich im Internet spotten*; [14]drawing – *Zeichnung*; [15]rumour – *Gerücht;* [16]wilting – *welkend*; [17]weak – *schwach*; [18]get lost – *sich verirren/verlieren*; [19]ruin – *ruinieren, zerstören*; [20]distance – *distanzieren*; [21]furious – *wütend;* [22]though – *trotzdem, dennoch, aber*; [2]
[3]observe – *beobachten;* [24]distraught – *verzweifelt*; [25]pluck up the courage – *allen Mut zusammennehmen;* [26]guilt – *Schuld(gefühl)*; [27]have the guts – *sich trauen, den Mut haben;* [28]forgive – *vergeben*

TB 6 p. 88

5 High school groups

a) Look at the five photos of typical groups in American high schools. Decide which group you would like to join.

b) Get together with the other students who have chosen the same group. Tell each other why you chose that photo. Then note down what you consider typical of the young people in the photo. Refer to clothes, interests, lifestyle, music etc. Report your results back to the class.

I chose / decided on this group because … | It has similar interests / clothes to me, for example … | This group appealed to me most because … | I could not imagine joining any of the other groups because … | …

1

2

3

4

5

c) Read the blog on page 37. Match the photos from a) to the different high school groups described in the blog and explain your decision to a partner.

TB 6 p. 88

6 A blog about high school groups

a) Read the blog on page 37. Certain rhetorical devices are used in the descriptions to make them more entertaining. Find more examples of the following rhetorical devices in the blog.
- repetition e.g. "They tend to be … and they tend to be …" (ll. 36–39),
- exaggeration e.g. "entire world revolves around sports" (ll. 23/24),
- alliteration e.g. "comfortable, casual clothes" (l. 41).

b) Choose the adjective which you think characterizes the tone of the descriptions best. Give reasons for your choice.

serious | light-hearted | humorous | ironic | neutral | critical | matter-of-fact

c) The tone of a piece of writing will often reveal the author's attitude towards his subject. Describe what the author's attitude towards school groups appears to be in the blog.

The author appears to approve / disapprove of … | The author seems to have a critical / neutral attitude towards school groups because …

So there's one question people from outside the USA always ask me: Are high school students divided into groups? Well, it's not exactly like in the movies, but here are the typical, general STEREOTYPES at my high school. But don't forget – the only way to really find out what someone is like is to talk to them and get to know them. They can and will surprise you.

Popular girls/cheerleaders: They will be at the top of the social ladder as far as fashion and looks go. What they lack in brains they make up for in hair products. They'll gladly gossip about anyone in order to make themselves look better. They are very outgoing and must always look like they are in love. Popular girls are involved in almost everything and often get to be cheerleaders. Cruelty is the order of the day with them, as beastliness and bullying are quite common.

Jocks: Typically these are muscly types, who are sometimes also good-looking. Their entire world revolves around sports and they demand special privileges in return for success on the sports field. They love what they do and are extremely confident, despite the pressure on them. The whole school is counting on them to win that title! Jocks are also not exactly known for their intellectual interests. If they are good athletes, bad grades don't matter because they will go to college on athletic scholarships.

Geeks/nerds: While geeks and nerds have been and can be separated into two categories, I'll put them together. They tend to be the people that actually care about their education and they tend to be brainy. As a result they are outside the ranks of popularity. Expect these people to wear comfortable, casual clothes and expect them not to spend much time thinking about their physical appearance. Geeks are more likely to have a 'cooler' character than nerds, whereas nerds may be more fanatical about things.

Fine arts kids: The fine arts kids are those students who are very interested in the arts. They like to draw, sing or perform in other artistic ways. Members of this group are creative and have many different clothings styles. They use color, art, piercings and other forms to express themselves and tend to have a more extravagant appearance.

Anime / manga fans: Members of this group are passionate about Japanese pop culture. They are passionate about animated series, passionate about films, passionate about graphic novels and passionate about other artwork. The anime / manga fans tend to spend a lot of time online in order to experience and share their passion.

d) Work with a partner.

1 First, each partner should note down the different groups of students at your school.
2 Compare your lists and write down the attributes of each group.
3 Discuss to what extent school groups in Germany are similar to those described in the blog.

TB 6.1 p. 105

7 A book blurb

Look at the book cover and read the blurb. Talk about whether or not you would like to read the book. Give reasons.

Maya is an 8th grader who describes herself as someone at the bottom of the social ladder at 'pretty much the lowest level of people at school who aren't paid to be here'. One day her mother finds a rather dated book from 1952, *Betty Cornell's Teenage Popularity Guide.* She suggests that Maya should follow the advice in the book and write about what happens. Maya embarks on a great experiment and follows Betty's advice on dieting, make-up, fashion etc.

This book doesn't appeal to me at all because … | The concept of this book sounds interesting but / because … | The cover would put me off reading this book because … | It could be quite exciting to find out … | On the one hand …, on the other hand … | I prefer to read … | Personally, I find this subject … | …

TB 6.1 p. 105

8 Popular

a) One of the last chapters in Betty Cornell's book is about meeting new people and making new friends. Read the extract below and speculate on what Betty's book might have advised Maya to do.

b) Describe how Kenzie views the consequences of Maya's plan and comment on her reaction.

For this first day, I sit with my regular, Social Outcast group during lunch. I listen politely to another story about how Kenzie's mother is stressing her out.
"Look, Kenzie, you know how I'm moving next year?" I say when she pauses for breath.
"Mhm."
"Well, I want to meet lots of new people before I go. I'm going to sit at different tables, and say "hi" to everyone. You know, make friends."
"What the hell? You're going to break the status quo! Ruin the social ladder! Destroy all the things that hold this world together!"

c) Read what happens when Maya puts her plan into action on page 39 and decide which description best sums up the events. Explain your choice and say why the other descriptions are less appropriate.

This extract from the memoir *Popular: Vintage wisdom for a modern geek* by Maya van Wagenen, published in 2014, …

- **A** describes how Maya abandons her social outcast friends.
- **B** describes how Maya tries to act like a popular student.
- **C** describes what happens when Maya plucks up the courage to join the popular group for lunch.

CHALLENGE Looking different

(1) Today is the day. I've been working up to this moment all month long. All year, for that matter. Today I sit with the jocks, the most popular people at our school: the highest of the Volleyball Girls and Football Faction all together at one table.

Here goes.

(2) The bell for lunch rings, and I slowly pull myself out of my desk and drag my feet down the hall towards the cafeteria. I can hear the blood pounding against the inside of my skull. My fingers shake as I try to remember everything I've learned, what's truly important in making friends.

I sit down across from a Volleyball Girl.

"Hey, Maya, what's up?" she asks, smacking her neon-pink chewing gum.

"Hey, Cristine, can I sit here today?"

"I guess."

"Thanks."

(3) Carlos Sanchez stumbles in with his buddy Pablo, singing "The Lion Sleeps Tonight". Badly. An onlooker would describe them as drunk, but they did the same thing during third period, so I'm not surprised.

He glances at me. I freeze and force myself to smile, even though I think I'm going to be sick.

"What's up, Maya?" He rejoins the song, then jumps back.

"Holy crap! Since when do *you* sit with *us*?"

(4) I try to stop my voice from shaking.

"I've sat with tons of people." I point to the tables around the lunchroom. The group seems impressed.

A football guy at the end of the table leans forward to see me. "Why?"

I relax a little. "For fun. Anyway, I'm moving to Georgia and –"

"WHAT! YOU'RE MOVING?!" Carlos Sanchez shouts loud enough for the entire cafeteria to hear.

"My dad got a job at a university there."

"But, you make our school look all smart and stuff. And now we're just gonna look dumb!"

Carlos Sanchez will miss me, too! Am I dreaming?

Some of the boys get into an argument about who will miss me most. [...]

(5) Someone from the nearby Choir Geek table hears the commotion, looks up, and sees me sitting at the most popular table at school. Her eyes widen, and she pokes one of her friends. They both gawk. One of them mouths, "What the hell?!"

I smile. Soon all the choir girls are staring at me.

I feel like a princess on a float. So I just smile and wave. The whole Popular Table is talking to me, competing, even, for my attention.

(6) As the bell rings on another successful lunch, I get up. One of the Football Faction members leans over to me.

"Don't sit at the gangster table. They're scary."

I'm shocked at his warning. "I already sat with them. They just don't speak much English." He shakes his head and disappears.

(7) When I get into the hall, all the choir girls surround me. "What were you doing?" they ask.

"I've sat with everyone. They weren't too bad."

"But the jocks are terrifying!"

"Maya, you're amazing!"

"You're so brave!"

"You've got some serious balls, man."

Wow, I mean ... Wow. I've never been considered brave, or even bold. Now, I have "serious balls".

I practically soar down the hall to my next class, but a question keeps bringing me back to reality: Why is everyone so scared of one another?

d) Read the extract again and note down briefly what happens in each section (1–7).

Example: 1. One day Maya decides to have lunch with the most popular kids at school.
2. When the bell rings, she ... and asks Cristine if ...

TB 2d p. 109

1 Meatless Monday

a) Read this information. What is it about? Sum it up in two sentences.

The school programme Meatless Monday has existed in the city of Baltimore, USA, since 2009. Every Monday students have vegetarian dishes instead of meat for lunch. Why meatless? Some experts say that eating a lot of meat can lead to different illnesses like heart disease and cancer, whereas eating a lot of vegetables can help to avoid health problems. If we all had meat-free Mondays, we would help to improve the environment – and the living conditions of animals because there would be fewer factory farms. The programme has been a great success for some time now. It is becoming more and more popular worldwide – not only at schools.

b) Read what some people think about meat-free Mondays at schools. Who can you agree with? Whose arguments do you think are good?

1. It's stupid. Nobody should tell me what to eat. If I want to become fat and ill … well, that's up to me. I love meat and can't do without it. My brother thinks meat-free Mondays are great though. He wants to lose weight and really cares about his health. My brother has eaten less meat since he started his diet. Now he hopes that our school will soon introduce meat-free Mondays.

2. It's OK. Our cafeteria doesn't serve meat on Mondays. I feel better and I've discovered that I like broccoli … and I can concentrate better.

3. My school cafeteria decided to start this programme. At first I thought it was going to be awful. But it's good actually. I don't eat breakfast at home. So lunch at school is my first meal of the day – and on Mondays it's really healthy, which is important.

4. It's good. I wish they'd stop serving meat all week – not just on Mondays. I've been a vegetarian for seven years. It's important to eat healthily and care about the environment. My sister hasn't eaten anything but burgers since she was 12. She's 16 now and she's overweight.

5. I really like meat. Since I was little I have loved eating all kinds of meat dishes. I think it's stupid that schools are thinking about meatless Mondays.

c) What do you think about Meatless Monday? Write your opinion.

… is a very important issue today. | I think / believe … | As I see it, … | I absolutely agree / disagree with … | In my opinion … | It is important to consider … | Another important point is … | All in all, I would say that … | That's why I think … | …

Writing your opinion

1. Make a pros and cons list or note down examples and reasons for your opinion.
2. Present your opinion in a structured order. Include examples and reasons.
3. Don't use informal language, e.g. short forms or colloquial language.

2 Going vegan?

TB 6 p. 110

a) Read the website. Take notes for pro and con arguments about veganism.

Pros

An improved health potential
Vegan diets are cholesterol-free and low in saturated fat. If you're at risk for chronic diseases such as heart disease or cancer, this could be an ideal diet for you. Just be sure to discuss it with your doctor before you take the plunge.

An increase in antioxidants
A vegan diet is full of antioxidant-rich foods like vegetables, fruits, beans, legumes, and more. Antioxidants are important because they have the ability to protect your cells from free radicals caused by a number of things including pollutants in the air such as tobacco smoke and radiation.

A lifestyle choice
Many people choose to adopt the vegan diet because of their love for animals and their desire for animals to live a humane life.
In addition, vegan values include concern for the environment, as a vegan lifestyle often supports sustainable agriculture and reduces the carbon footprint associated with meat-producing operations.

Cons

Another reason to read food labels? A seemingly vegan food might just contain ingredients that aren't suitable for a vegan diet. Take for example gelatin, which is derived from meat, and whey, which is derived from milk. Whey can be found in many granolas, breads, and more.

Sticking to a strict diet
In addition to not eating meat, fish, or poultry, vegans steer clear of any animal products and by-products. That includes honey, eggs, dairy, cosmetics derived from animal products, and more. If you choose to go vegan, you may have a hard time choosing from the menu when dining out.

Potential vitamin and mineral loss
There are vegan sources for most nutrients, but it might be a challenge to consume enough of them. Take iron and vitamin D for example. Vitamin D isn't typically found in the vegan diet, but can be obtained through exposure to sunlight. When people think iron, they typically think meat.
But beans and leafy greens are also good sources, and you can increase iron absorption by coupling them with foods that are rich in vitamin C.
You'll also need to supplement vitamin B12, which only occurs naturally in animal foods.

A lack of protein
A healthy diet should incorporate some form of protein into every meal. Since vegans forego typical protein sources like meat and eggs, they have to incorporate it through different means. If you're thinking about going vegan, it's time to stock up on plant-based protein such as soy, quinoa, lentils, and beans. And beware of overly-processed meat substitutes, which can be packed with sodium and preservatives. Check labels before opting for that frozen tofu burger!

b) Have a discussion with a partner. One of you wants to go vegan and one of you is against it. Use the arguments in the pro and con list.

TB 10 p. 112

3 Helping the climate?

a) What do you think are advantages of a vegetarian diet?
What are disadvantages?
Brainstorm with a partner and take notes.

A vegetarian diet	
advantages	disadvantages
- better for your heart	- less protein
- ...	- ...

b) Read the article on pages 43 and 44. Then answer the questions.

1. Which disadvantages are listed in the article if more people would become vegetarians?
2. What are the main issues of food wastage according to the article?
3. What are the author's suggestions to ensure better sustainability?
4. Do you agree with the author's suggestions? How does this article make you feel about food?

c) Do you think it would be possible for you or your family to reduce food wastage?
Collect ideas and write a short text about what you could do or what you already do to avoid throwing away food.

What we can do to avoid throwing away food
- plan meals for the week
- buy frozen food
- ...

... is a very important issue today. | The issue of ... is more important than ever before. |

Firstly, I think / believe we could reduce food wastage by ... | To avoid throwing away food it is important to ... |

In my opinion ... | I think so because ... | It is important to consider ... | Another important point is ... |

All in all, I would say that it is possible to ... | That's why I think ... | ...

Is a vegetarian diet really more environmentally friendly than eating meat?

Wayne Martindale, The Conversation UK 26.01.2017

Beef from Brazil, avocados from Mexico, lamb from New Zealand, wines from South Africa and green beans from Kenya – food shopping lists have a distinctly[1] international flavour.

And with many questioning the sustainability[2] of importing so much food from so far away, we are beginning to ask if switching to a vegetarian diet to cut emissions caused by meat production is as sustainable as one might think.

The influence of the global trade[3] of food on local diets and cultural choices has exploded over recent years. Food supply chains[4] operate[5] globally and deliver rural produce to nearly 4 billion people now living in cities and towns.

It was this principle that established[6] the world's first agricultural research station some 150 years ago when the founders of Rothamsted saw the potential of the agricultural land surrounding London to supply[7] a growing urban population. In the 21st century, the whole world can be your bread basket.

Many are conscious[8] of what they eat – both from a health and environmental perspective. But what is the impact of this? We're increasingly encouraged to eat less meat to tackle climate change. And meat consumption, in the European Union at least, has reduced and stabilised at around 42m tonnes over the last 15 years.

There are also now new labels for different types of meat eaters: flexitarians (only eat meat sometimes) or the reducetarian (aim to eat less meat) that reflect the ways different groups are trying to cut down.

But what about all those fruit, vegetable and staples crossing the globe – can we really label them as more sustainable than eating meat? The growth of ethical food purchases[9] now make up close to 10% of grocery purchases in the UK, which is double that of tobacco.

But in addition to the impact of air miles, global land and resource use determine the sustainability of the food we eat – food production can destroy or displace natural resources in order to supply growing demand[10].

Changing land use to expand avocado production in Mexico, for example, is displacing the rainforest. Or the devastating impact of non-certificated palm oil, used in food but also a whole host of other products. And then there is the issue of food wastage[11].

Measuring the sustainability of food

However, the first thing we need to be able to do is measure the environmental impact of the food we eat. We can do this for different food supply chains using carbon footprinting[12] methods. The difficulty is that consumers choose foods based on what they like – and this frequently changes but rarely[13] considers the impact of climate change. From this we can say that a vegetarian diet does deliver a decreased carbon footprint. But it also shows us that food miles and global distribution can be the least of our problems.

This is because food wastage can be up to 20% of food purchases and food losses across the supply chain can be far greater than this. Food waste in turn increases

[1]distinctly – *deutlich, klar*; [2]sustainability – *Nachhaltigkeit*; [3]trade – *Handel*; [4]supply chain – *Lieferkette*; [5]operate – *betreiben, bedienen*; [6]establish – *schaffen, herstellen*; [7]supply – *versorgen, beliefern*; [8]conscious – *bewusst*; [9]purchase – *Kauf*; [10]demand – *hier: Nachfrage*; [11]wastage – *Verschwendung*; [12]carbon footprint – *CO_2-Bilanz-*; [13]rarely – *selten*

the carbon footprint which counters the positive gains[14]. And perishable fresh fruit and vegetables are more likely to be thrown away than fresh meat and fish.

So is vegetarian really best?

Ultimately, we cannot say if eating a vegan or vegetarian diet versus a meat one is any better for the environment. This is because all can be appropriate if production systems are sustainable, there is no waste and positive health outcomes are achieved. There are clearly trade-offs in choosing foods. Air freighting[15] of green beans from Kenya into the UK was seen as unsustainable because of air miles but it also supports up to 1.5m people and livelihoods in some of the poorest regions of Sub-Saharan Africa.

It's not just meat that increase greenhouse gases. Rice – produced on 163m hectares, around 12% of the global arable area – has one of the greatest plant carbon footprints because it produces a lot of methane.

But a fall in production of rice is not only unlikely, it could also disrupt greenhouse gases held in the soil. But there are different ways to do things – draining off paddies at particular times in the growing season[16], for example. Or using different fertilisers[17] or rice varieties that are less susceptible[18] to the heat.

The best way forward?

Consumers need to understand trade-offs and to keep up to date[19] on information of what is best to buy. It is important to spot food trends, for example, and project any sustainability impacts. The number of gluten-free products available is doubling year-on-year[20] in Europe and the US. This has resulted in an increase in the consumption of plant proteins from beans and lentils. These kinds of foods are arguably more eco-friendly than meat but – whatever your thoughts about gluten-free eating – it will change how protein crops are distributed globally and may divert pulses or increase the price of them for countries such as India that depend of non-livestock proteins.

Sustainability certifications have changed how we shop, giving us guidance[21] on ethical purchases including sustainable fishing, rainforest produce and so on. This is one way to make sure that what you eat is less damaging and/or helps sustain livelihoods and good agricultural practices. But it is day-to-day[22] food waste – both at home and in supply chains – that can make any diet unsustainable whether you choose to be vegan, vegetarian, a meat eater or a combination of these. Different preservation formats can reduce food waste to zero. In the case of frozen food we know food waste can be halved compared with fresh foods – less of it is thrown away. Despite what you might think, frozen compares well to fresh and can be just as nutritious[23]. We all choose foods based on what we like, what we can access and what we can afford. But continued surveillance[24] and interest in sustainable production will mean we can buy produce we know has a better supply chain. There isn't currently a certification that shows food produced with less waste (there should be), but we can aim to cut down our own and keep up with suppliers who show better commitments[25]. We might have an avocado – but maybe not five in a week. And of course we can source[26] more food locally and seasonally as well as considering preserved options if we want to cut down on air miles. Like eating less meat, there are ways to make your footprint better.

[14]gain – *Gewinn*; [15]air freighting – *Flugtransport*; [16]growing season – *Anbausaison*; [17]fertiliser – *Dünger*; [18]susceptible – *empfänglich*; [19]keep up to date – *auf dem neuesten Stand bleiben*; [20]year-on-year – *Jahresvergleich*; [21]guidance – *Anleitung*; [22]day-to-day – *alltäglich*; [23]nutritious – *nahrhaft*; [24]surveillance – *Überwachung, Kontrolle*; [25]commitment – *Engagement, Verpflichtung*; [26]source – *beziehen*

4 Fight the climate crisis

TB 5 p. 116

a) Read the article. What is it about?

b) Answer the questions.
1. What was Sophie Mitchell's dream? What did she do?
2. How did the idea develop? Note down the different steps.
3. What does Sophie do to inform people about how to live more eco-friendly?
4. What does Sophie say about the importance of zero-waste stores?
5. What do people think about a zero-waste lifestyle?

c) What do YOU think about a zero-waste lifestyle? Write down your opinion. Use your own ideas and arguments taken from the text.

HOW ONE PERSON IS HELPING TO FIGHT THE CLIMATE CRISIS

Max Harris, Mon 9 Sep 2024

28-year-old Sophie Mitchell always knew that she had to make an impact[1] when it came to fighting against environmental[2] issues. She followed in her father's footsteps[3] and became an agricultural[4] business student at Michigan State University. However, she could not have imagined the direction[5] in which the fight against environmental issues would take her.
In 2019, Sophie was lucky enough to get the chance to study abroad in Germany. During her time at the Humboldt University in Berlin, she came across a zero-waste store. As she walked in, she was taken aback[6] by the fact that – as the name suggests – there was absolutely zero waste in the entire store. You could bring containers and fill them up with food such as cereal, pasta and nuts. You could buy plastic-free refills for shampoo and body wash. You could even buy bamboo toothbrushes, or buy milk in glass bottles which you then returned to the shop to be refilled.

At the time, Sophie had never come across[7] anything like this in her home town of Michigan in the US. That's when she got the idea to open her own zero-waste store there. In her final year at university, she began to plan.
With the help from one of her former business lecturers[8], she came up with a business plan and presented it to the bank to get funding[9]. Sophie managed to receive a loan[10] of $6,000 with which she opened an online shop to sell zero-waste products.
At the beginning, she ran[11] her online shop from her own living room. This went really well and she was soon able to make her wish come true: she opened up[12] her own store in the heart of Michigan.

[1]make an impact – *Auswirkungen haben*; [2]environmental – *ökologisch, die Umwelt betreffend*; [3]footstep – *Schritt*; [4]agricultural – *landwirtschaftlich*; [5]direction – *Richtung*; [6]take aback – *verblüffen, schockieren*; [7]come across – *hier: stoßen auf*; [8]lecturer – *Dozent'in*; [9]funding – *Finanzierung; hier: finanzielle Förderung*; [10]loan – *Darlehen, Kredit*; [11]run – *hier: führen, betreiben*; [12]open up – *hier: eröffnen, schaffen*

We spoke to Sophie about how she turned her dream into reality.
Sophie, you started with just a dream of opening your own store. Tell us about it.
It was a difficult start, but I spoke to one of my business lecturers when I was still a student. She suggested that I come up with five unique products that I could sell in the future. She recommended that I first start off[13] small at the university and work my way up. This meant that I began with a limited[14] target audience[15], before moving it to an online shop, and then eventually[16] a real store. I contacted the university and asked if I could have my own stand at an information fair[17] taking place for new students. They accepted. So I took my products, which included hairbrushes made out of bamboo as well as shampoo bars, and started having conversations with students who were passing by my stand. I talked to a lot of people about the products and about how they can help our planet in the long run[18].

And you haven't stopped talking since then …
(laughs) Yes, that's right. Because I enjoyed talking to people and showing them ways to combat[19] climate change with little things, I started holding online courses on zero-waste and how to do it successfully. I also created simple online guides which companies can purchase[20] for some tips and tricks. My weekly blog posts on zero-waste do really well, too. All of which helped towards opening my own zero-waste store …

That sounds fantastic! What role would you say zero-waste stores play in our world?
Zero-waste stores educate people about eco-friendly products and makes them more accessible[21]. One of the major problems is that you don't tend to find such products in mainstream superstores or other places that people often shop at, so people are unaware[22] that they could buy their usual shopping with more eco-friendly alternatives. What I find so exciting is that people often realize how convenient[23] the products that zero-waste stores sell are and it really makes a big change. For example, did you know that bamboo products are naturally antibacterial[24]? That makes bamboo particularly appealing[25] for hygiene products.

What would you say are some common misconceptions[26] when it comes to a zero-waste lifestyle?
The main misconception that I always like to prove wrong[27] is that buying eco-friendly products is much more expensive than buying "standard" products in a store. That's simply not true. Sure, sometimes it may be true – but it isn't the case for all products. I often find that you can buy refills of things like shampoo for less money than if you buy a one-use[28] bottle of shampoo. What people forget about or don't realize is that the number of customers who shop at zero-waste stores actually affects our prices: the more customer support we have, the larger the quantities[29] are that we can order which in turn makes the prices cheaper. […]

[13]start off – *beginnen, anfangen*; [14]limited – *begrenzt, eingeschränkt*; [15]audience – *Publikum*;
[16]eventually – *irgendwann, schließlich*; [17]fair – *hier: Messe*; [18]in the long run – *langfristig*; [19]combat – *bekämpfen*;
[20]purchase – *kaufen, erstehen*; [21]accessible – *zugänglich, erreichbar*; [22]unaware – *nicht bewusst*;
[23]convenient – *zweckmäßig, praktisch*; [24]antibacterial – *antibakteriell*; [25]appealing – *attraktiv, reizend;*
[26]misconception – *falsche Vorstellung/Auffassung*; [27]prove sth wrong – *jdm beweisen, dass er/sie Unrecht hat*;
[28]one-use – *Einweg-;* [29]quantity – *Menge, Quantität*

5 A different view

TB 8 p. 119

a) Read Jon Negroni's blog. What do you find interesting or funny about it? Talk to a partner.

b) What do you think about the article? Do you agree that going back to the Earth is a bad thing for the humans of Wall•E? Why? Why not? Write a short text.

The Humans of 'WALL-E' Were Probably Better Off[1] Without Him

by Jon Negroni / April 15, 2015

Have you ever seen Pixar's WALL-E? [...] Let's recap the story. WALL-E is set 800 years in the future. In this universe, Earth becomes incredibly overpopulated[2] by the year 2105, with 200 billion humans contributing to an environmental disaster for obvious reasons. In response[3], a world-dominating organization called Buy n Large (BnL) pledges[4] to clean up the mess, though it's heavily implied[5] it's mostly their fault, and they send all humans to space on executive cruise ships called "starliners." But after only five years, BnL decides to abandon[6] the planet completely because the air has become toxic[7]. Anyway, humans remain in space unbothered for 700 years, which is when the movie's plot begins with WALL-E. When a probe named EVE arrives to find hospitable life, WALL-E falls in adorable robot love with her, and when she returns to deliver the plant-life she found, WALL-E frantically[8] follows her. WALL-E ends up on Axiom, one of many starliners running in a lifestyle "loop." The humans there have been raised from birth to support and trust BnL and it's routines for their entire lives. The robots satisfy[9] all of their needs, and life is pretty much perfect in their minds, even though they do nothing for themselves. It's a strange setup because you'd think the people on Axiom would grow bored and feel stifled[10], but in contrast, they seem completely intent, until WALL-E arrives and causes a chain of events that leads to their return to Earth. This brings me to the main point: **The people of Axiom are incredibly nice, well-functioning people.** Not once do you see a human on Axiom acting spoiled[11] or rude. Instead, they're incredibly polite, especially when they meet WALL-E for the first time. John and Mary are two great examples. They're not used to robots having a personality, and when they meet WALL-E, they are very positive and nice to him. You'd think they'd treat him terribly, but instead they befriend[12] him and get eerily[13] excited when they see him again. The humans we see have friends, romantic relationships, and excellent living accommodations. The screens they view everything through

[1]be better off – *es besser haben*; [2]overpopulated – *überbevölkert*; [3]in response (to) – *als Antwort (auf)*; [4]pledge – *versprechen;* [5]imply – *hier: andeuten*; [6]abandon – *verlassen;* [7]toxic – *giftig*; [8]frantically – *wie wild, verzweifelt*; [9]satisfy – *befriedigen, stillen, erfüllen*; [10]stifle – *unterdrücken*; [11]spoiled – *verwöhnt*; [12]befriend sb – *sich mit jdm anfreunden*; [13]eerily – *unheimlich*

are translucent[14], so they have no shame in letting other people see what they're working on. Even life expectancy[15] isn't a problem. When we see the panel of past Axiom captains, you can see that all of them live well over 100 years. When the current captain of the ship becomes enamored[16] with Earth, he appears to have the joy of a child. He's incredibly optimistic, and in many ways, one of the central heroes of the film when it comes down to it.

In some of the final scenes, we see the humans showing a lot of empathy[17] for WALL-E and EVE, even though most of them have no idea what's going on. They cheer for the captain when he's fighting Auto, and John and Mary don't hesitate[18] to risk their lives for the babies falling down the platform.

What caused humans to be this nice?

Well, BnL apparently did. The society created by this "loop" of never-ending pleasure created a culture of interestingly polite humans, contrary to[19] the spoiled rich kid syndrome you'd expect to see.

So was what WALL-E did for them ... for the best? If he had never followed EVE, the humans would still be on the Axiom, but when the movie closes, the humans have returned to Earth. It's depressing[20], but history repeats itself. Though we see shots of life rebuilding[21] itself peacefully, won't humans just make the same mistakes again and damage Earth completely this time? It's tricky because the movie is clever about how it makes you hate BnL, despite it being the invention of the very humans we sympathize[22] with. Pixar overtly[23] makes the conditions of the Axiom both horrific and enticing[24] at the same time, but few people walk away from it thinking the humans made a mistake. From a storytelling perspective, it's genius on Pixar's part. They present the humans in a way that makes us want the best for them. If they had made the humans spoiled and insufferable, we wouldn't care about them as much as we do by the end. But the weird side-effect[25] of this characterization is that Pixar is unintentionally[26] saying that BnL's methods created a better society than the one we already have. We know it's better because Pixar is intentionally saying the society we have is what caused the problems emphasized in the film.

So, here's the question: Were the humans better off living in a society that made them the best they could be personally and socially? Or is living on Earth too important to ignore? I'm not convinced either way, to be honest. Sure, the effects of gravity make you a blob[27] dependent[28] on a chair, but then again, it's an awesome chair.

In Axiom's society, there's no crime from what we see. Everyone has their needs met. There's likely no poverty, racial injustice, or food shortages. It's utopia, but we think it sucks[29] because the people aren't skinny. Isn't that a little messed up[30] when you think about it?

[14]translucent – *lichtdurchlässig*; [15]life expectancy – *Lebenserwartung*; [16]enamored (with) – *begeistert (von)*; [17]empathy – *Einfühlungsvermögen, Empathie*; [18]hesitate – *zögern*; [19]contrary to – *im Gegensatz zu*; [20]depressing – *deprimierend*; [21]rebuild – *wieder aufbauen*; [22]sympathize – *Verständnis haben, Mitleid haben*; [23]overtly – *unverhohlen, offen*; [24]enticing – *verlockend*; [25]side-effect – *Nebenwirkung*; [26]unintentionally – *unabsichtlich*; [27]blob – *Klumpen*; [28]dependent (on) – *abhängig (von)*; [29]suck – *ätzend sein;* [30]messed up – *verkorkst*

Still, the captain makes a good point when he says, “I don’t want to survive, I want to live!” But does everyone on Axiom want that, or is it just the result of one man who wants to impulse buy[31] something he read about on the Internet? It’s hard to say. Of course, I’m not saying Axiom would be the best for me or you. We’re accustomed to[32] bike rides, trampolines, and Taylor Swift concerts. But if you told me there was a way to solve all of Earth’s problems in exchange for a few extra pounds, I’d have a hard time[33] saying no.

[31]impulse buy – *einen Spontankauf machen*; [32]be accustomed (to) – *gewohnt sein (an)*; [33]have a hard time (with sth) – *(mit etw) Probleme haben*

6 Who is to blame?

TB 10 p. 120

a) Look at the cartoons. Talk about what you can see. What are the cartoons trying to say?

b) What can YOU do to protect the planet? Have a discussion in class.

“Tonight, an in-depth look at what each of us can do to help conserve electricity.”

it is important to do our part to help the environment son....

TB 1d p. 139

1 A gap year

a) Read the website and find out what a gap year is.
b) Your friend who doesn't speak much English has found this website too. He/She wants to understand what it is about. Write a summary about it in German.

Gap years: the Essential Guide

A gap year is a year's break between school and starting to work or going to university. Gap years can offer the opportunity to experience a range of things you wouldn't be able to in your ordinary life.

Travel

Lots of people enjoy travelling during a gap year. It is a great way for you to become more confident. It could be the first time that you live away from home and you will have to look after yourself, cook, clean and manage your money.
Travel is expensive, so you'll need to save beforehand[1] and to find ways of travelling cheaply, such as camping. Many people spend part of a gap year working to earn enough to travel. This experience can also look good on your CV or personal statement. However, travel will need to be relevant to be useful: for example, if you want to study politics, then travelling to a place with a political situation you are interested in and learning more about it first-hand[2] might be useful. Just going on holiday is less likely to impress universities or employers. Typical skills gained from travelling include: independent thinking, budgeting, problem-solving, forward-planning and good communication. Travelling, particularly in countries with a very different culture, can help you to become more independent and learn how to cope on your own.
Whilst it is safer to travel with friends, some people do travel on their own.

Volunteer

Volunteering can be a cost-effective[3] way to see the world, or make a difference in your home country. There are many different charities that will offer you the chance to do a long-term[4] voluntary placement[5].
To see some examples, look online.
They offer volunteering opportunities in England, anything from planting trees to running after-school clubs for children.
Alternatively, you can find something a bit further afield.

Learn

Spending your gap year studying might seem like missing the point, but it can be valuable[6].
For example, you might:
Learn to drive
Learn a new language
Learn practical skills like DIY

Work

OK, it doesn't sound that fun, but working during your gap year could be one of the most rewarding things you do. If you've got time to spare[7] before university, why not use it to build some valuable skills that will look great on your CV, and to earn some cash?
You may have to choose between unpaid work experience, which may be more beneficial[3] for your CV, and work that pays but is less relevant to your career. However, you can split your time between this, and it's always worth looking for paid work in the area you're interested in even if you don't expect to get it.

[1]beforehand – *vorher, im Voraus*; [2]first-hand – *aus erster Hand*; [3]cost-effective – *kostengünstig*; [4]long-term – *langfristig*; [5]placement – *hier: Stelle, Praktikum*; [6]valuable – *wertvoll*; [7]have got time to spare – *Zeit (und Muße) haben*; [8]beneficial – *nützlich, vorteilhaft*

2 The pros and cons of a gap year

TB 1d p. 139

a) Read the article about the pros and cons of a gap year. Would any of these change your mind about taking a gap year? Take notes and discuss with a partner.

b) Can you imagine taking a gap year? Why? Why not? What would you do? Give reasons.
Example: I can't imagine taking a gap year. I want to ... I would be worried ...

Gap years: Pros and cons

Between school or college and university is a good time to take time out[1], whether it's to earn some money for your studies, get work experience, travel the world or volunteer. (You don't even have to worry about applying to university at the end of the year: you can apply before your gap year and take 'deferred[2] entry', which means you have an offer but it's postponed[3] for a year.) But gap years aren't for everyone, so it's important to consider the pros and cons before making a decision.

Pros

- The experiences you gain can make you better prepared for university, both academically and socially
- It's probably the longest 'holiday' you will ever be able to take in your life - taking long breaks[4] will be harder once your career starts
- You can use some or all of the time to earn money for university, taking the pressure off your finances
- You can learn new skills
- You get the chance to experience life away from home before starting university
- Volunteering gives you the opportunity to help people
- Both volunteering and working will provide valuable work experience
- If you're feeling dedicated[5], you can get ahead[6] on preparations[7] for your course
- If you didn't get the grades in one of your A-levels, you can retake it and reapply while using the rest of your time to do something else

Cons

- If you want to travel or take part in an organized gap year programme, it could be expensive
- There may be changes to your course or your student finance package during your year off
- If your friends from home are all going to uni, your social life could dry up[8]
- Unless you revise, you can forget a lot in a year that would be useful to your course
- If you've got a university offer and haven't already agreed to defer your place, you could be putting your place at risk
- If you don't get organised, you may end up spending your gap doing nothing but watching TV. Not great for the CV!

[1]take time out – *sich eine Auszeit nehmen*; [2]defer – *verschieben, aufschieben, aussetzen*; [3]postpone – *verschieben*; [4]take a break – *eine Pause machen*; [5]dedicated – *engagiert*; [6]get ahead – *vorwärtskommen*; [7]preparation – *Vorbereitung*; [8]dry up – *hier: versiegen*

TB 5 p. 142

3 Working abroad

a) Read the article. What is it about?
b) Read the article again. What are the advantages of working abroad for some time? Take notes.
c) Tell somebody who hasn't read the text about the article.

Work Experience Abroad

Work experience is a great way to get some hands-on[1] experience in a particular job that you are maybe interested in and want to find out more about. It can give you an idea of what it is like to do the job, and it can also be a great addition[2] to your CV. But have you ever considered doing work experience abroad? Going abroad to get some work experience is a fantastic way to make you stand out from other applicants when you come back to your home country and start looking and applying for jobs (unless you stay out there, of course!).

Work experience abroad can mean many things – it can be working on a social work project in the Himalayas, working as an au pair in America, or on a financial project in Senegal. The possibilities are nearly endless, and you are definitely going to find something that interests you. People who have work experience abroad on their CVs usually stand out from the crowd because employers[3] consider them to be open-minded[4] and generally more employable[5]. It also shows that you are courageous: You decided to leave the comfort of your home country and try out something new in a brand new country. That isn't something that everybody could easily do!

Another advantage of doing work experience abroad is that you will likely be exposed to different languages and multicultural environments – both at work and in your personal life. It shows that you can communicate and get on with people from different backgrounds, which can be quite challenging. It highlights[6] your willingness[7] and flexibility when it comes to trying new things and adapting[8] to new tasks, places and people. So, when you are thinking about your next step, why don't you consider taking a gap and going abroad to gain some valuable work experience?

[1]hands-on – *praktisch*; [2]addition – *Ergänzung*; [3]employer – *Arbeitgeber/in*; [4]open-minded – *aufgeschlossen*; [5]employable – *vermittelbar*; [6]highlight – *hervorheben*; [7]willingness – *Bereitschaft*; [8]adapt (to) – *(sich) anpassen (an)*

TB 5 p. 142

4 Transferable[1] skills

a) Read the article on page 53. What are transferable skills? Explain in two sentences.
b) Do you think the article helps people who want to find their first job? Why? Why not? Write a short comment.

Transferable skills: How to use your summer job to start a career

By Amelia Butterly, Newsbeat reporter

It can be hard to write a CV, if you're still at the start of your career and don't think you have much experience. This is where transferable skills are very useful. A summer job, whether it be working in a shop, waiting[2] on tables or working in a call centre, can be great experience for gaining new skills. *Newsbeat* has spoken to career advisors[3] to explain how to work out what transferable skills you have and how to write about them in a CV.

What kinds of transferable skills might you have?

"Communication is going to be one of the main ones, whether you work in a bar or a call centre," says Rachel Locke, an advisor from the National Careers Service." Quite often you have to deal with difficult customers or difficult situations so I think being able to negotiate[4] situations like that requires[5] tact and diplomacy on the part of the individual." Working in a restaurant would also help with your communication skills, Sarah Frend from Inspiring Futures says. "You'd have to work alongside[6] other people," she says, which would demonstrate teamwork. "You might even take on a leadership role by running a section of the restaurant and directing other people." Other examples she suggests include things like working on a shop till demonstrating numeracy[7] and IT skills. Labouring could show stamina and a "mature" outlook when it comes to considering your own and other people's health and safety.

How do you show off your transferable skills on a CV?

"It's important to be very concise[8] but very specific at the same time," says Ms Locke. "It's getting the right balance of having those applicable skills and demonstrating it with an example each time, so not just saying you've got this skill, but give an example of when you've used this and how you demonstrated it and what it resulted in as well." She says that for each application you must have a "specific" CV which matches the job description. Pick out the "key points" from the description and link it to your "previous, relevant experience".

What if you've never had a summer or part-time job before?

"Even from studying, there are a lot of skills that young people would have picked up," says Ms Locke. You may have organisation and time management skills from managing assignments[9], communication skills from speaking and writing in class, or problem solving and analytic skills from working on projects. She says skills like working in a group or leading people can come from "extra curricular activities[10]" such as captaining a sports team.

What's the best bit of advice for writing your CV?

"Don't churn out the same one time after time," says Ms Frend. "Adapt your CV to every application. Some jobs are going to have certain skills that are going to be more important to them. "The clue should be in the job description, where you can see what it is they really want. "Tick them [skills] off in the order that they come on the specification[11]."

[1]transferable – *übertragbar*; [2]wait (on tables) – *als Kellner/in arbeiten*; [3]career advisor – *Berufsberater/in*; [4]negotiate – *aushandeln*; [5]require – *brauchen, erfordern*; [6]alongside – *neben, zusammen mit*; [7]numeracy – *rechnerische Fähigkeiten*; [8]concise – *hier: knapp*; [9]assignment – *Aufgabe*; [10]extra curricular activities – *Aktivitäten außerhalb des Stundenplans*; [11]specification – *hier: Beschreibung*

TB 9 p. 146

5 Job interview mistakes

a) Read the article.

The 13 most common job interview mistakes

Want a new job? Here are the mistakes made time and time again[1] by candidates, sourced from serial employers

BY REBECCA BURN-CALLANDER, ENTERPRISE EDITOR

There are many reasons that candidates luck out[2] during interviews. They may not have the right qualifications for the job. Or, in worst cases, they are downright incompetent.
But if you have all the skills you need for the role (on paper, at least) and you're still failing to impress your prospective employer, you could be unwittingly[3] committing one of these interview crimes.

1. Showing off[4]
Despite what you might see on The Apprentice[5], employers are rarely impressed by outrageous claims or displays of ego. Make sure all your bragging[6] is justified, says Philip Oldham.

2. Failing to do your homework
In today's information age, there is absolutely no excuse for knowing nothing about the company you are applying to work for. "This includes at a minimum doing your research on what it is and does," says Jack Lion Heart.

3. Making up answers
Inflating[7] your expertise is a quick way to alienate your interviewer. If you don't know the answer to a question, it's better to be up front about it. "When asked a question they don't know the answer to, a lot of people try to guess, or try to bullsh*t the interviewer, or start going through facts they know that don't really answer the question," says Jadin Attar. "Don't do that. Just state clearly that you don't know.

4. Forgetting your manners[8]
"I once had a candidate who was respectful to all his male interviewers and totally rude to all his female interviewers," says Wong. Equally, directing all your answers to the most important person in the room instead of to the person who asked the question is disrespectful. Swearing[9] and crass comments are also no-nos.

5. Asking no questions
"I have always found it fascinating that so many [interview candidates] never ask me anything," says Pieter D Roussouw.
"A job interview not only enables the potential employer to assess your skills and suitability[10] but it also enables the interviewee[11] to assess if this company is in fact a good employer, compatible with your needs." "At least ask something about what you'll actually be doing and who you'll be doing it with," says Henry. "Job postings very rarely give a sense of[12] what an actual day in the job will feel like."

[1]time and (time) again – *immer wieder*; [2]luck out – *Schwein haben, hier: Pech haben*; [3]unwittingly – *unabsichtlich*; [4]show off – *angeben*; [5]The Apprentice – *Name einer Fernsehsendung*; [6]brag – *prahlen*; [7]inflate – *übertrieben darstellen*; [8]manners – *Manieren*; [9]swear – *fluchen*; [10]suitability – *Eignung, Tauglichkeit*; [11]interviewee – *Befragte/r, Interviewte/r*; [12]give a sense of … – *einen Eindruck von … vermitteln*

6. Apologising unnecessarily
This is the quickest way to undermine[13] yourself in front of an employer, according to Steven Mason. He warns that "apologising for yourself, for others, for your answers, for your appearance, for anything" could make you look weak. "Apologise if you accidentally elbow someone in the mouth, not because you don't know the answer to a question or you don't agree with them or anything else outside of basic etiquette. Be who you are. Confidently."

7. A bad handshake
"I won't cancel you outright for a bad handshake, but it doesn't do you any favours[14]," says Henry. "They're simple to learn, and prove that you're deliberate and thoughtful about how you present yourself."

8. Failing to explain what you will bring to the party
According to Ed Weinstein, this problem is particularly true of recent graduates. "They use their cover letter to explain what our position can do for them instead of explaining what they can do for us."

9. Moaning[15] about your current employer
"You're not running from somewhere but to somewhere," says Steve Everhard. "No employer wants to feel that you are joining them because it's better than where you are." Instead, show that you are excited by the opportunities the new firm represents.

10. Using 'yes' or 'no' answers
"What is most impressive is the candidate that expounds[16] on the answer, showing how he understands the material," says Brian Feeny.

11. ... Unless the interviewer requires a 'yes' or 'no' answer
"The most common issue I've had when interviewing people is when they ramble on[17] forever," says Tracey Croughwell Saenz. "I really appreciate when a candidate listens to the question, and answers it thoughtfully and concisely. Don't try to squeeze in every great thing about yourself when you're asked a specific question."

12. Trite[18] or practiced answers
Beware answers that seem too rehearsed – or that you've pulled straight out of an "idiot's guide to interviews"-style manual. "If I ask a candidate, "What is your biggest weakness?" and they mention something that's actually a skill like "perfectionism" or "working too hard", it lacks insight and is a feeble attempt to impress," says Esha Krishnaswamy.

13. Dressing sloppily[19]
"I interviewed a candidate for a programmer position years ago," says Frederic Gray. "He came into the interview sporting a scraggly beard, unkempt hair, and a dirty T-shirt. I asked him, 'Is this the outfit you expect to wear at work?' He responded that he expected to get paid for performance, not to be a fashion model (or words to that effect). "I said that if we ever got a job for a programmer that never had to set foot in the office we would certainly call him back in, then dropped his resume in the trash and thanked him for coming in."

[13]undermine – *untergraben, schwächen*; [14]not to do sb/oneself any favour – *jdm/sich keinen Gefallen tun*; [15]moan – *hier: sich beschweren, klagen*; [16]expound – *darlegen, näher ausführen*; [17]ramble on – *schwafeln*; [18]trite – *platt, abgedroschen*; [19]sloppy – *schlampig*

b) Your German friend is preparing for a job interview and needs help. Write him/her an email and give him/her advice. Explain five to six tips from the article you think are the most important in German.

Hallo ...,
Ich habe einen Artikel zu Jobinterviews gelesen. Es wird geraten, ...

TB 5 p. 150

6 Teenagers spending money

a) Do you worry about money? Why? Why not? Talk to a partner.
b) Read the interview on the website. What do you think about Will Clarkson's advice?
c) Imagine you want to help a friend who is having problems because he / she spends too much money. What would you tell him / her?
Work with a partner and write a dialogue.
d) Write a blog entry for other teenagers. Give advice on handling money.

Money is something that teens and their parents often fight about. We had a chat with Will Clarkson who is an expert in how to handle money. Here's what he said:

Thanks for talking to us today, Will!
Our first question is: What got you interested in helping teens with their money?

Will: Well, I'm a personal coach and I help people to worry less, be more happy and to achieve big goals. I found that my clients who are parents usually complained about their children and money. They often said that their kids thought money grew on trees! On the other side of things, I also volunteer for a local scouts group for young kids, and the kids often complain about their parents – "they just don't understand!". That is what got me interested and why I decided to do some research on the topic of teens and money. There are books out there on managing money that claim there is just one way to achieve financial independence from your parents. But that's really not true – there are so many different ways.

OK, interesting. So, the big question is: Why is saving money important to a teenager?

Will: That's the thing – many teens don't actually think saving is important. As soon as they get some cash, many of them are already planning what they are going to spend it on. They want to use and enjoy it right now, and they're not bothered[1] about the future. Then again, some teens do prefer watching their bank balance[2] grow and being aware[3] of where every cent is going. This may sound like the most sensible solution, but it can be just as problematic: These people can become cheapskates[4], refusing to spend any money and not taking time to enjoy the opportunities that money can bring. Rather than simply saving for a rainy day and then never actually spending a single cent, you should at least consider ways to save your money in a way that somehow produces money. For example, you could look at saving accounts[5] at different banks with good interest rates[6], or look more into investing into shares[7] or stocks[8]. Just make sure you read up on all of that stuff before diving into it. There is a lot of information out there on the Internet. Your parents or another adult you trust may be able to help you.

[1]be bothered – *(auf etw) achten, (mit etw) beschäftigt sein*; [2]bank balance – *Kontostand*; [3]be aware of sth – *sich einer Sache bewusst sein*; [4]cheapskate – *Geizkragen*; [5]saving account – *Sparkonto*; [6]interest rate – *Zinsrate*; [7]share – *Anteil*; [8]stocks – *Aktien*

Search

Can you give us some ideas about how teenagers can better budget their money?

Will: Sure. I have five things I'd like to mention:

1. It's good to understand how you see money. It doesn't matter if you're a spendthrift[9], if you refuse to spend a single cent, or if you're anywhere between those two extremes. Work out what your mindset[10] is and try to use that to your advantage. If you know your mindset, you can deal with your budgets better.
2. You should set a financial goal that is slightly challenging, but doable[11]. Setting an unrealistic goal is the first step to failure. If you have a manageable goal in mind, you will think twice about spending money on extra fries for your lunch!
3. Make sure that the present is just as important as the future. Yes, you should prepare for the future when you are planning your finances. But the present shouldn't suffer through that. So don't set a budget that is too restrictive and prevents you from enjoying today.
4. Try to learn from others. If your parents or another trusted adult in your life is financially comfortable, ask them what they did to get where they are today. Remember: Being financially comfortable does not mean being extremely rich! It means that you have enough money to pay your rent or mortgage[12] as well as other necessities like food, while having a little money on top to enjoy extra things in life, such as any hobbies you have.
5. Be creative. If you can't afford something, think of how you can afford it. Could you take on an extra shift at your part-time job? Is your birthday coming up soon so you could ask for a little money as a gift? Could you borrow some money from your parents and pay them back next month? Or perhaps you have some old items at home, like books or video games, that you could sell? You only have a chance of succeeding if you try!

Fantastic! Those are great tips. Do you have any final pieces of advice before we finish?

Will: Sure. The thing I say the most to both parents and teenagers is that money is not worth fighting about. It comes and it goes. At the end of the day, true wealth[13] is what you have when your money is gone. If you are a kind person with no money, you will be a kind person when you have an abundance[14] of income[15]. If you're a horrible person with no money, then you will also be a jerk[16] if you have lots of money.

Having said that, many people argue that there are more important things in life than money. I agree with that to a certain extent, but it would be a lie to say that money is not important at all. In today's age, money is needed for a lot of things, such as health and social activities. It's important to keep the balance. Make sure you manage your money well, but don't let it be your top priority. The worst thing you can do is to stop enjoying life because you're too worried about your bank balance going down.

[9]spendthrift – *Verschwender/in*; [10]mindset – *Denkart, Mentalität*; [11]doable – *machbar*; [12]mortgage – *Hypothek*; [13]wealth – *Reichtum, Wohlstand*; [14]abundance – *Fülle, Vielzahl*; [15]income – *Einkommen*; [16]jerk – *Blödmann, Trottel*

TB 9 p. 152

7 The influence of influencers

a) What do you know about influencers? Make notes.
b) Read the article and find out more about influencers and advertising. Which information is new to you? Take notes.
c) Answer these questions.
1. Why are influencers attractive to the advertising industry?
2. How does influencer marketing work?
3. What are the dangers for teenagers?

d) What do you think about influencers and their advertising?

The influence of influencers

When we think about influencers, we think about people online who we follow. Usually, they have a specific thing that they focus on. One famous example is PewDiePie who creates videos of video game playthroughs[1], among[2] other things. Another example is Rocio Cervantes who is a popular makeup influencer and struggles with acne – making her more likeable and down to earth[3].

But where does the term[4] "influencer" come from? It's simple: Influencers are people who try to influence[5] people to buy and use certain products or services[6].

Influencers are very interesting for the advertising industry. Influencers can use social media to upload a new video of their latest gadget[7] or must-have eyeliner, and suddenly their video is watched by tens, hundreds, thousands of people – depending on[8] how popular they are. But what makes influencers different to advertisements you see at the bottom of websites or on TV? This is where it gets interesting. Influencers are just like you and me – normal people who live a normal life. Their photos and videos show this. They might take videos in their home or car. This makes them more relatable[9]. If we find someone relatable, there is more chance that we will be interested in them and admire[10] them. And if they are eating a snack they say is delicious, then you'll want to try it, too. It is like getting a recommendation[11] from a friend.

[1]playthrough – *Durchlauf*; [2]among – *unter, zwischen*; [3]down to earth – *bodenständig*; [4]term – *Ausdruck*; [5]influence – *beeinflussen*; [6]service – *hier: Dienst, Hilfe*; [7]gadget – *Gerät, technische Spielerei*; [8]depending on – *je nachdem*; [9]relatable – *jd, zu dem man einen Bezug hat*; [10]admire – *bewundern*; [11]recommendation – *Empfehlung*

Of course, influencers don't do all of this for free[12]. They earn money in a variety of ways. For example, they may have a special link or a code that you can enter[13] when you purchase an item they are advertising and get money from that. Another method is "product placement[14]". This is when a company pays the influencer to have a certain item in their videos, or the company sends the influencer a present and asks them to film themselves opening it. Fans can even pay money to send special messages in a live chat, buy the influencer's merchandise[15], or even pay money at big events to have a selfie with their favourite influencer!

This all sounds fantastic, but let's not forget about the problems. It can be hard to achieve the things mentioned above. On big video platforms, an influencer needs at least 1,000 subscribers[16] to start earning money, and they require 4,000 watch hours in the past year (which means that fans need to have watched more than 4,000 of their videos in total). It can take a lot of time to reach this goal, but you need to spend a lot of time on it if you want to make a living wage[17]. It is estimated that you earn $60,000 a year when you have one million subscribers. Imagine how long it takes to reach one million subscribers!

Let's take a step back and think about the people who are influenced – you and me. Influencers are paid to advertise products. So does that always truly mean they like the product themselves? Or are they just doing it for the money? We can easily be influenced by these people because they feel like close friends. It is a very clever method of advertising. Their recommendations can feel very real and honest. In fact, sometimes we are influenced without realising it. That's why influencers require a small disclaimer[18] to let their fans know that they are being paid to advertise something – that is something you should watch out for.

One thing here is important: This all doesn't mean that you should never trust anything that an influencer says. It's more important to understand how influencers earn money so that we can take more logical decisions when they advertise something.

So the next time you're scrolling through your timeline and you come across[19] a video from your favourite influencer talking about a certain product, make sure to stop and think why they are advertising it. Don't fall for[20] the advertisement immediately[21], but think about whether you really need the product – or whether you just think you need it because the influencer, who seems like your close[22] friend, says you do.

[12]for free – *gratis, umsonst*; [13]enter – *hier: eingeben, eintrage*; [14]product placement – *Produktplatzierung*; [15]merchandise – *Handelsware*; [16]subscriber – *Abonnent/in*; [17]living wage – *Existenzminimum*; [18]disclaimer – *Erklärung*; [19]come across – *hier: stoßen auf*; [20]fall for sth – *auf etw hereinfallen*; [21]immediately – *sofort*; [22]close – *hier: eng*

Bildquellen

|Alamy Stock Photo, Abingdon/Oxfordshire: Tholpady, Ashok 45.1. |Alamy Stock Photo (RMB), Abingdon/Oxfordshire: Christine Osborne Pictures 16.1; DPK-Photo 20.1; Johnson, Stephen R. 36.1; Long, Suzanne 13.3; MBI 36.5; nagelestock.com 3.1; Oeland, Ingo 18.1; RubberBall 36.2; Steffen Binke 13.2; Travelscape Images 51.1; Urmas Haljaste 21.2; WaterFrame 12.1. |Bridgeman Images, Berlin: 16.2. |CartoonStock.com, Bath: Chris Slane 32.3; Christine Anderson 49.3; Kim Wark 32.4; Marty Bucella 32.2; Mike Baldwin 32.1, 49.1; Tim Whyatt 49.2. |Colourbox.com, Odense: Scigelova 21.1. |Imago Editorial, Berlin: HBL Network 23.1. |iStockphoto.com, Calgary: Juanmonino 42.1; mocker_bat 36.4; Terriana Titel; visual7 11.1. |mauritius images GmbH, Mittenwald: World Pictures 14.2. |Penguin Random House LLC, New York: Popular: Vintage Wisdom for a Modern Geek (A Memoir)" von Maya Van Wagenen 38.1. |Picture-Alliance GmbH, Frankfurt a.M.: m69/ZUMA Press 17.2; www.flyingdoctor.org 14.1. |Shutterstock.com, New York: CandyBox Images 25.1; Chulov, Dmitry 17.1; Dimitrov, Strahil 22.1; G-Stock Studio 58.1; Mandy Godbehear 36.3; monkeybusinessimages Titel; Prostock-studio 59.1; Race, Dan 52.1; Shift Drive 53.1; Steve Allen 8.1; Syda Productions 57.1. |stock.adobe.com, Dublin: Brivio, Marco 12.2; KopoPhoto 24.1; manuta 45.2; Nejron Photo 56.1; Tandem Stock 13.1; vkph 41.1.

Textquellen

S. 15: "Mercy flight through the storm" auf https://www.flyingdoctor.org.au/about-the-rfds/stories/mercy-flight-through-storm/ © Royal Flying Doctor Service, 27.04.2017;

S. 16/17: http://www.survivalinternational.org/tribes/aboriginals, © Survival International, London, 18.10.2022;

S. 18/19: "Follow the rabbit-proof fence" by Doris Pilkington, © University of Queensland Press, Brisbane, Queensland, 2002;

S. 23–25: "Taking sports to the extreme" by Jane E. Brody, August 15, 2016, 5:45 AM, auf https://archive.nytimes.com/well.blogs.nytimes.com/2016/08/15/taking-sports-to-the-extreme/ From The New York Times. © 2023 The New York Times Company. All rights reserved. Used under license.

S. 27: "The legend of New Zealand" auf https://www.newzealand.com/int/feature/the-legend-of-new-zealand/ © New Zealand Government, Wellington, 10.11.2022;

S. 28/29: "Aotearoa or New Zealand: has the moment come to change the country's name?" auf https://www.theguardian.com/world/2022/aug/11/aotearoa-or-new-zealand-has-the-moment-come-to-change-the-countrys-name, © Guardian News and Media Ltd 2023, Eva Corlett, Wellington, 10.08.2022;

S. 30: "True friend" Text by Jeannie Renee Lurie © Walt Disney Music USA, Universal Music Publishing GmbH;

S. 31: "We're going to be friends" by Jack White © Peppermint Stripe Music/Universal/MCA Music Publishing GmbH, Berlin;

S. 38/39: Excerpt(s) from "Popular: Vintage Wisdom for a Modern Geek" © Maya Van Wagenen, Dutton Children's Books, an imprint of Penguin Young Readers Group, a division of Penguin Random House LLC, New York, 2014;

S. 41: "The pros and cons of a vegan diet" by Candice Graham auf https://healthscopemag.com/health-scope/the-pros-and-cons-of-a-vegan-diet/ © HealthScope Magazine, Chattanooga, Tennessee, October 15, 2015;

S. 43/44: "Is a vegetarian diet really more environmentally friendly than eating meat?" auf https://theconversation.com/is-a-vegetarian-diet-really-more-environmentally-friendly-than-eating-meat-71596 © Wayne Martindale, The Conversation UK, January 26, 2017;

S. 47–49: "Retronalysis: The Humans of 'WALL-E' Were Probably Better Off Without Him" auf https://jonnegroni.com/2015/04/15/the-humans-of-wall-e-were-probably-better-off-without-him/ © Jon Negroni, 15.04.2015;

S. 50: "Gap years: the Essential Guide" auf https://www.brightknowledge.org/education/gap-years-the-essential-guide © brightknowledge.org; Brightside CAN Mezzanine 7 - 14 Great Dover Street London SE1 4YR;

S. 51: "Gap years: Pros and cons" auf https://www.brightknowledge.org/education/gap-years-pros-and-cons © brightknowledge.org; Brightside CAN Mezzanine 7 - 14 Great Dover Street London SE1 4YR;

S. 53: "Transferable skills: How to use your summer job to start a career" auf http://www.bbc.co.uk/newsbeat/article/33960410/transferable-skills-how-to-use-your-summer-job-to-start-a-career © Amerlia Butterly, BBC, London, 17.08.2005;

S. 54/55: Auszüge aus "The 13 most common job interview mistakes" by Rebecca Burn Callander and Rebecca Burn Calland auf https://www.telegraph.co.uk/finance/jobs/11237738/The-13-most-common-job-interview-mistakes.html © Telegraph Media Group Limited 2014.